FARTHER AFIELD

FARTHER AFIELD

BY MISS READ

Illustrated by J. S. Goodall

Academy Chicago Publishers

Published in 1991 by
Academy Chicago Publishers
213 West Institute Place
Chicago, Illinois 60610

Copyright © 1974 by Miss Read

Reprinted by special arrangement
with Houghton Mifflin Company

Printed and bound in the USA

Library of Congress Cataloging-in-Publication Data

Read, Miss.
    Farther afield / by Miss Read ; illustrated by J.S. Goodall
       p.   cm.
    ISBN: 0-89733-371-3 (paper)
    I. Title.
  [PR6069.A42F35 1991]
823' .914–dc20   91-32510
                                    CIP

For Audrey and Jack
with love

CONTENTS

Part One

A Visit To Bent

Part Two

Farther Afield

Part Three

Return To Fairacre

Part One

A Visit to Bent

1 End of Term

'WHEN do we come back?' said Joseph Coggs.

He stood close by my chair, rubbing the crepe sole of his sandal up and down the leg. A rhythmic squeaking, as of mice being tortured, had already turned my teeth to chalk. I turned to answer the child, anxious to put us both at ease, but again I was interrupted.

In the midst of the hubbub caused by end-of-term clearing-up, Patrick and Ernest had come to grips, and were fighting a silent, but vicious, battle.

Without a word, I left Joseph, moved swiftly into the arena, and plucked the two opponents apart with a practised hand. With a counter-movement I flung them into their desk seats where they sat panting and glowering at each other.

Despite all the modern advice by the pundits about irreparable damage to the child's ego, I continue to use out-dated but practical methods on an occasion like this, and find they work excellently. Sweet reasoning will not be any more effective with two young males in conflict than it will with a dog-fight on one's hands. The first objective is to part them; the second to find out why it happened.

In this case, a revoltingly dirty lump of bubblegum had been prised from under a desk, and both boys laid claim to it.

Both are well-nourished children, from decent homes,

whose mothers would have been as disgusted as I was by this filthy and aged sweetmeat finding its way into their hands, let alone their mouths.

I held out my hand, and Patrick put the clammy object into it. For once, it landed in the waste-paper basket, without mishap, and the incident was closed.

Patrick and Ernest returned to their desk-polishing, much refreshed by the tussle, and at last I found time to answer Joseph Coggs.

'Term begins on September 5th,' I told him.

He sighed.

'It's a long time,' he said mournfully.

'A *very* long time,' I agreed, beaming upon him.

No matter how devoted, dedicated, conscientious and altogether *noble*, a teacher is, I feel pretty sure that each and everyone feels the same sense of freedom and relief from her chains when the end-of-term arrives.

And of all end-of-terms, the most blissful is the end of the summer term, when six weeks or more stretch ahead, free of time-tables, bells, children and their parents. Six weeks in which to call your soul your own, to enjoy the garden, to think about next year's border plants, and of stocking up the log shed, even, perhaps, a little house decoration and tidying cupboards, although the thought of Mrs Pringle over-seeing the latter operation cast a cloud upon the sunny scene.

Mrs Pringle, school cleaner and general factotum to Fairacre School, sometimes obliges by giving me an extra hour or two on Wednesdays. I greet her offers with mixed feelings. On the one hand, the house certainly benefits from her ministrations, but her gloomy forebodings and her eloquent dissertations on the deplorable way I manage my house-keeping affairs are enough to dash the stoutest heart.

I had already determined to assist Mrs Pringle in her 'bottom-ing', as she terms a thorough cleaning, and to behave in as kind and Christian a manner as was possible under extreme provoca-tion. If, as I knew from experience, Mrs Pringle's needling became intolerable, I could always put some cheese, biscuits and fruit in the car, with the current book and that day's crossword puzzle to solve, and drive to one of the nearby peaceful spots, far from Mrs Pringle's nagging tongue and the reek of unnecessarily strong disinfectant.

'After all,' I told myself, 'I can take quite a lot of Mrs P. It's when Mrs Hope is dragged up and flaunted before me that I crack.'

Mrs Hope was the wife of a former headmaster, and had lived in the school house as I do now. She must have had a dog's life, for her husband drank, and she found solace in unceasing work in the little house.

'From dawn to dusk, from morning till night,' Mrs Pringle has told me, far too often, 'Mrs Hope kept at it. Never without a duster in her hand, and anybody invited to tea was met on the doorstep, and offered a clothes brush and a pair of slippers so as not to soil the place.'

'I shouldn't think many returned.'

'No, that's true,' said Mrs Pringle thoughtfully. 'But then Mrs Hope was *very* particular who came to the house.'

This was a side-swipe at me whose door stands open for all to enter.

Mrs Hope, so I am told, was always at the wash-tub before seven, twice a week, and even scrubbed out the laundry basket each time. Like Mrs Tiggywinkle she was 'an excellent clearstarcher', and naturally *nothing*, not even heavy bedspreads and curtains, was ever sent to the laundry.

'Mrs Hope would have scorned such a thing, and anyway laundries don't get the linen really clean. And, what's more they use *chemicals*!'

If she had said that the dirty linen was prodded by devils with pitchforks, she could not have sounded more scandalised.

The introduction of Mrs Hope into any conversation was usually breaking point for me, and I could foresee many alfresco meals whilst Mrs Pringle was obliging.

There are many places within a quarter of an hour's drive from Fairacre which make glorious picnic spots. There are hollows in the downs, sheltered from the winds, where the views are breathtaking, and the clouds throw little shadows like scurrying sheep on to the green flanks of the hills.

There are copses murmurous with cooing wood pigeons, and fragrant with damp moss and aromatic woodland flowers. But my favourite spot is by the upper reaches of the River Cax, before it wanders into Caxley, and threads between the rosy houses to find its way eastward into the Thames.

Here the wild cresses grow in the shallows, their white flowers dazzling against the darker water. Little water-voles splash from the bank into the stream, stopping occasionally to nibble a succulent shoot, or to chase another of their kind. And here too a heron can be seen upstream, standing like some shabby furled umbrella, dark, gaunt and motionless upon the bank.

It is here, particularly on a sunny day, that its magic works most strongly. It is the 'balm of hurt minds'. No human being is in sight. No human habitation distracts the eye. The slow-moving water flows at the same pace as it has always done, sheltering and giving life to fish, plants and insects. Thirsty bees cling to the muddy brink. Dragon-flies dart, shimmering, across the surface, and the swallows swoop to drink. Below, in the murk, among the drifting water weeds, the dappled trout lie motionless. Life, in its infinite forms, pursues its unchanging course, timeless and unhurried, and a man's cares fall from him as the things that matter – sunshine, moving water, birds and small beasts – combine to cast their spell upon him.

I was snatched from my reverie by Linda Moffat's voice.

Where, she was demanding, should she put the two dozen or so fish-paste jars she had just collected and washed 'off of the nature table?'

'Never use "off of",' I replied mechanically, for the two thousandth time that term. A losing battle this, I thought resignedly, but one must soldier on. 'Having a lend of' or 'a borrow of' is a similar enemy, while 'she never learnt me nothing' or 'I never got teached proper', pose particular problems to those attempting to explain the niceties of English usage.

'Try the map cupboard,' I suggested, watching the child transferring a black smear from her hand to a freshly-starched linen skirt. Poor Mrs Moffat, I thought compassionately, and the child at home for six weeks!

'Miss,' shouted Ernest, above the din, 'it's home time.'

'Two minutes to finish clearing up,' I directed, fortissimo.

Within three, they rose for prayers. The class-room was bare, ready for Mrs Pringle's ministrations during the coming week, and the wastepaper basket was overflowing.

'Hands together, eyes closed.'

I waited until the seats had stopped banging upright, and the fidgeting had stopped.

'*Lord, keep us safe this night,*
Secure from all our fears,
May angels guard us while we sleep,
Till morning light appears.
Amen.'

If this was taken at a more spanking pace than usual, why not? Ahead stretched freedom, fresh air, bathing and fishing in the infant Cax, wrestling and jumping, rejoicing in growing strength, and, no doubt, eating all day long – ice-cream, potato crisps, biscuits and loathsome bubble-gum, in an endless stream.

'Make sure you take *everything* home, and enjoy your holidays. When do you come back?'

'September the fifth, miss,' they chanted.

'Very well. Good afternoon, children.'

'Good afternoon, miss.'

And then began the stampede to get out into the real world which was theirs for six whole weeks.

I remained behind for a few minutes, locking drawers and cupboards, and retrieving a few stray papers to add to the load in the wastepaper basket.

I locked the Victorian piano. How much longer would it hang together, I wondered? The tortoise stove stood cold and dusty now, but Mrs Pringle's hand and plenty of blacklead would prepare it for the autumn term. There would be the familiar battle I supposed, about '*the right day*' to light it, Mrs Pringle playing for time, whilst I pleaded, cajoled, and finally ordered, the stove to be lit.

But what did that matter now? 'Seize the moments as they pass,' said the poet, I intended to follow his sound advice, and locking the school door, emerged into the sunshine.

There was a welcoming chirrup from Tibby as I entered the front door of the school house. She was at the top of the stairs, yawning widely, her claws gripping the carpet rhythmically as she stretched.

Plain Wilton carpet costs an enormous amount of money, as I discovered when I was driven to replace the threadbare stair carpet last year. Tibby has seen to it that the top and bottom stair are generously tufted, much to the horror of Mrs Pringle, and to my lesser sorrow.

It is sad, I know, to see such maltreatment of one's furnishings, but one must look realistically at life. Either one has no cat and plain Wilton, or one has a cat and tufted Wilton. I prefer the latter.

Tibby, I knew, had just arisen from her resting place on my eiderdown – another habit which Mrs Pringle deplores.

'Cats' fleas cause cholera', she told me once with such conviction that I almost believed her. She followed up the attack with a vivid account of someone she knew who had allowed their child – or maybe it was their second cousin's child – to bite the skin of a banana. The result was a rash, diagnosed on the spot by the doctor as leprosy, and the child was never seen again by the family.

Although I did not believe a word of this cautionary tale at the time, so downright was Mrs Pringle's manner whilst telling it, that I still find myself opening a banana with careful fingers and making sure that the children do the same. The cholera I have decided to ignore. A school teacher's life is too busy to follow up every precaution suggested, and in any case, Tibby, I tell Mrs P. robustly, has no fleas.

The cat sprang down the stairs and accompanied me into the kitchen, watching the kettle being filled, the tray being set, and all the familiar routine leading to a few drops of milk in a saucer for her, as I drank my tea.

A quarter of an hour later, my second cup steaming beside me, I watched her as she lapped. Eyes half-closed in bliss, her pink tongue made short work of the milk.

'We've broken up, Tib,' I told her. 'Broken up at last.'

I leant back and thought idly about the hundred and one domestic affairs I must see to. There was Mr Willet to consult about a load of logs. And then I had promised the vicar I would play the organ whilst the regular organist, Mr Annett, had his annual holiday. I must check the dates. And the sitting room curtains were in need of attention. Ever since their return from the cleaners, the lining had hung down a good three inches, so that even I had been irritated by their slip-shod appearance.

Then I really ought to tidy all the drawers in the house. The kitchen table drawer jammed itself stubbornly on the fish-slice every time it was opened. But where could the fish-slice go? And the paper-bag drawer had so many stuffed into it that half of them had fallen over the back into the bottling jar cupboard below.

Never mind, I told myself bravely, with all this time before me the place would soon be in apple-pie order. Why, I might even get round to labelling all those holiday prints of yesteryear before I clean forgot the names of the places.

It was pleasant lying back in the armchair reviewing all the jobs waiting to be done, confident that all would be accomplished in the golden weeks that lay ahead. I should tackle them methodically and fairly soon, I told myself, stretching as luxuriously as Tibby. No need to rush. And later on I should take myself for a short holiday somewhere pleasant – Wales, perhaps, or Northumberland, or the Peak District. Or what about Dorset? Very attractive, Dorset, they said . . .

Near to slumber, I basked in my complacency. The teapot cooled, the cat purred and a bumble bee meandered murmurously up and down the lavender hedge outside.

Months later, looking back, I realised that that blissful hour was the high-light of the entire summer holiday.

2 Struck Down

DAWN breaks with particular beauty on the first day of the holidays, no matter what the weather. On this occasion, the sun fairly gilded the lily, rousing me with its beams, and dappling the dewy garden with light and shade.

I took my coffee cup outside, and sniffed the pinks in the border. This was the life! Even the thought of Mrs Pringle, due to arrive at 9.30 for a 'bottoming' session, failed to quench my spirits.

Across the empty playground stood the silent school. No bell would toll today in that little bell-tower. No jarring foot would jangle the metal door scraper. No yells, no screams, no infant wailings would make the air hideous. Fairacre School was as peaceful as the graveyard nearby – a place of hushed rest, of gathering dust, given over to the little lives of spiders and curious field mice.

Not for long, of course. Within a few days Mrs Pringle would begin her onslaught. Buckets, scrubbing brushes, sacking aprons, kneelers, and a lump of tough yellow soap prised from the long bar with a shovel, with an array of bottles containing disinfectant, linseed oil and vinegar, and other potions of cleanliness, would assault the peaceful building under the whirlwind direction of Mrs Pringle herself. Woe betide any stray beetle or ladybird lurking behind cupboards or skirting boards! By the time Mrs Pringle's ministrations were over, the place would be as antiseptic as a newly-scrubbed hospital ward.

In the far distance I could hear sheep bleating and a tractor chugging about its business. A car hooted, a man shouted, a dog barked. The life of the village went on as usual. The baker set out his new loaves, the butcher festooned his window with sausages, the housewife banged her mats against the wall, and the liberated children beset them all.

Only I, it seemed, was idle, glorying in my inactivity as happily as the small ruffled robin who sat sunning himself on a hawthorn twig nearby. But such pleasant detachment could not last.

St Patrick's had long ago struck nine o'clock, and the crunch of gravel under foot now told of Mrs Pringle's arrival.

I sighed and went to greet her.

Mrs Pringle's black oil-cloth bag, in which she carries her cretonne apron and any shopping she has done on the way, was topped this morning by a magnificent crisp lettuce, the size of a football.

'Thought you could do with it,' she said, presenting it to me. 'I know you don't bother to cook in the holidays, and I noticed all yourn had bolted. Willet said you was to pull 'em up unless you wanted to be over run with earrywigs.'

I thanked her sincerely for the present, and the second-hand advice.

'Tell you what,' went on the lady, struggling into her overall, 'if you pull them up just before I go, I can throw them to my chickens. They can always do with a bit of fresh green.'

I promised to do so.

'Well, now,' said Mrs Pringle, rolling up her sleeves for battle, 'what about them kitchen cupboards?'

'Very well,' I replied meekly. 'Which shall we start on?'

Mrs Pringle cast a malevolent eye upon the cupboards under

the sink, those on the wall holding food, and the truly dreadful one which houses casseroles, pie-dishes, lemon-squeezers and ovenware of every shape and size, liable to cascade from their confines every time the door opens.

'We start at the top,' Mrs Pringle told me, 'and work down.' She sounded like a competent general issuing orders for the day to a remarkably inefficient lieutenant.

I watched her mount the kitchen chair, fortunately a well-built piece of furniture capable of carrying Mrs Pringle's fourteen stone.

'Get a tray,' directed the lady, 'and pack it with all this rubbish as I hand it down. We'll have to have a proper sort-out of this lot.'

Obediently, I stacked packets of gravy powder, gelatine,

haricot beans, semolina and a collection of other cereals and dry goods which I had no idea I was housing.

'Now, why should I have three packets of arrowroot?' I wondered aloud.

'Bad management,' snorted Mrs P. There seemed no answer to that.

'And half this stuff,' she continued, 'should have been used months ago. It's a wonder to me you haven't got Weevils or Mice. I wouldn't care to use this curry myself. That firm went out of business just after the war.'

I threw the offending packet into the rubbish box – a sop to Cerberus.

'Ah!' said Mrs Pringle darkly, 'there'll be plenty more to add to that by the time we've done.'

It took us almost an hour to clear all three shelves. Mrs Pringle was in her element, wrestling with dirt and disorder, and glorying in the fact that she had me there, under her thumb, to crow over. I can't say that I minded very much. Mrs Pringle's slings and arrows hardly dented my armour at all, and it was pleasant to come across long lost commodities again.

'I've been looking everywhere for those vanilla pods,' I cried, snatching the long glass tube from Mrs Pringle's hand. 'And that bottle of anchovy essence.'

'It's as dry as a bone,' replied Mrs Pringle with satisfaction, 'and so's this almond essence bottle, and the capers. What a wicked waste! If my mother could see this she would turn in her grave! Every week the cupboards were turned out regular, and everything in use brought forward and the new put at the back. "Method!", she used to say. "That's all that's needed, my girl. Method!" and it's thanks to her that I'm as tidy as I am today,' said my slave-driver smugly.

'My mother,' I replied, 'died when I was in my late teens.'

But if I imagined that this body blow would affect my sparring partner, I was to be disappointed.

'It's the early years that count,' snapped Mrs Pringle, throwing a box of chocolate vermicelli at my head.

I gave up, and we continued in silence until the cupboard was bare. Then I was allowed to retreat upstairs to dust the bedrooms whilst Mrs Pringle attacked the shelves with the most efficacious detergent known to man.

A little later, over coffee, Mrs Pringle gave me up-to-date news of the village.

'You've heard about the Flower Show, I suppose?' she began.

I confessed that I had not attended this Fairacre event on the previous Saturday.

'A good thing. There's trouble brewing. Mr Willet says he's writing to the paper about it.'

'Why? What happened?'

'You may well ask. Mr Robert won first prize for the best kept garden.'

This did not seem surprising to me. Our local farmer always keeps a fine display of flowers and vegetables.

'What about it?'

Mrs Pringle took a deep breath, so that her corsets creaked.

'Mr Roberts,' she said, with dreadful emphasis, 'has Tom Banks working in that garden three days a week – if working you can call it. And, what's more, he had all the farmyard manure at his beck and call. How can us cottagers compete with that?'

I saw her point.

'The Flower Show's never been the same,' said Mrs Pringle,

'since that fellow that worked up the Atomic got on the committee. Good thing he's been posted elsewhere, but the trouble
still remains. All this Jack's-as-good-as-his-master nonsense!
Don't you remember the outcry when he wiped out the
cottager classes? Said it was degrading to have two types of
entry. As though we bothered! If you does your own digging
and planting, you're a cottager. If you gets help, you're not. I
never could see why that man was allowed to question the ways
of the Almighty. "The rich man in his castle, the poor man at
his gate", says the hymn. And what's wrong with that, I'd like
to know? If there'd been a cottagers' class, as there always used
to be, then Mr Willet would have come first, and rightly so.
He's drafting a fair knock-out of a letter to the Caxley.'

I said I should look forward to reading it in next week's
'Caxley Chronicle'.

'Oh, I don't say it will be in that early,' said Mrs Pringle,
stacking our cups. 'So far it's only got as far as the first draft on
a page of Alice Willet's laundry book. But he's keeping at it.'

She replaced the lid of the biscuit tin.

'Mrs Partridge's niece goes back to London today. I should
think she and the vicar will be downright thankful. As far as I
can hear, the girl's done nothing but wash her hair and walk
about with one of those horrible transistors all day.'

'She's supposed to be a very clever girl,' I said, rising to the
absent one's defence.

'Being clever don't get you far,' sniffed Mrs Pringle. 'There's
some, not a hundred miles from here, who's passed examina-
tions and that, but don't know no more than that cat what's in
their cupboards.'

Reminded of her duties, she rose and removed the tray from
the kitchen table to the draining board.

'You'd be least bother to me,' she told me, 'if you made yourself scarce while I tackle that china cupboard. I don't trust myself to keep a civil tongue in my head while that's being bottomed, and I've never been one to speak out of place, I hope.'

She glanced at me sharply.

'I suppose you wouldn't have such a thing as some good white paper for lining the shelves when I've washed them?'

'As a matter of fact,' I told her with some pride, 'there's a roll of lining paper upstairs. I'll run up and get it.'

It was pleasant to dazzle Mrs Pringle with my efficiency for once, and I rooted about in the landing cupboard among boxes of stationery, stored Christmas tree decorations, and a mound of yellowing cuttings from magazines which I tried to deceive myself into calling 'Reference Material' although, in my honest moments, I knew full well I should never refer to them.

The roll of lining paper had managed to work its way to the very bottom of the cupboard, and right to the back behind a pile of box files dusty with age, and bearing such labels as 'Infant Handwork Ideas', 'Historical Costumes', and the like. I wouldn't mind betting that most teachers have just such a collection of junk tucked away, carefully garnered as an insurance against the future, and looked at only once in a blue moon, or else forgotten completely.

The cupboard was a deep one and by the time I had wriggled the slippery roll from behind the boxes, I was hot and dusty and had laddered one stocking. I struggled to my feet feeling quite giddy with my exertions.

I hoisted one of the dusty files under one arm. It contained, if I remembered rightly, some patterns for making simple lamp shades, and these might prove useful for handwork next term. I would go through the box at my leisure.

Mrs Pringle's lining paper began to behave like a telescope, the inside sliding out at remarkable speed. From being eighteen inches in length, the roll rapidly became thirty, and caught itself in the banisters as I took the first unsteady step downwards.

Everything happened at once. The heavy file slipped, the lining paper jammed, my ankle turned over with a crack, and the hall carpet rushed upwards to meet me amidst whirling darkness lit with stars. The latter moved into a circle, as though about to embark on 'Gathering Peascods'. Suddenly, they vanished altogether, and I wondered why so many bells were ringing.

When I came round I was sitting on the bottom stair with my face against Mrs Pringle's bosom.

It was enough to bring me rapidly to full consciousness.

'You bin and fell down,' said that lady reproachfully.

There seemed nothing to add.

Five minutes later, on the sofa, I found myself trying to control my chattering teeth and to assess the damage done.

Mrs Pringle, who had collected the papers strewn all over the hall, now surveyed me lugubriously.

'Well, you've made a proper job of it,' she told me, with some satisfaction. 'If you don't have a black eye by morning, I'll eat my hat. And something's not right with that ankle.'

'Sprained,' I said. 'Nothing more, but my arm feels strange.'

It hung down at approximately its usual angle, but felt queerly heavy.

'Could be broken,' Mrs Pringle suggested, about to investigate.

'Don't touch it,' I squealed. I lifted it carefully.

'I don't think it can be broken,' I said. 'I mean there aren't any bones sticking through the flesh, and it isn't a funny shape, is it?'

'Could still be broken,' replied Mrs Pringle, with conviction. 'You don't know much about it, do you?'

I admitted that I was entirely ignorant when it came to anatomy. All I knew was that I was shaking and cold and for two pins would have howled like a dog.

'I should like some brandy,' I said. 'It's in the sideboard.'

Leaning back, I closed my eyes and gave myself over to being a casualty. Hell, how that ankle hurt! It would be swollen to twice the size in an hour, that was sure, and heaven alone knew what was the matter with my right arm.

I took the proffered glass in my left hand and sipped the fire-water.

'Where's Doctor Martin this morning?' I asked. 'He'd better look me over, I suppose.'

'Wednesday,' said Mrs Pringle, seating herself heavily on the end of the sofa, far too close to my damaged ankle for my peace of mind. 'Wednesdays he's in Fairacre. He'll be at Margaret Waters sometime this morning, having a look at her bad leg. What a bit of luck!'

'Who for?' I said crossly. 'Oh, never mind, never mind, I'll ring there and leave a message.'

I struggled to my feet, screamed, and fell back on to the sofa again.

'It's The Drink,' said Mrs Pringle, in a voice of doom. I remembered that the blood of dozens of Blue-Ribboners beat in her veins, and regretted that I had allowed her to administer brandy to me, even for purely restorative reasons.

'No,' I managed to say, 'it's the ankle. Perhaps you would ring Miss Waters and ask her to see if Doctor Martin could call.'

She went into the hall, and I swallowed the rest of the brandy. It was such a solace in the midst of my increasing discomfort that, for the first time in my life, I began to understand why people took to the bottle.

I lay back and surveyed the room through half-closed eyes. A bump over my right eye was coming up at an alarming rate. Would it be the size of a pigeon's egg by the time the doctor arrived, I wondered? And why a *pigeon's* egg? Why not a hen's or a bantam's egg?

Objects in the room had a tendency to shift to the left when I looked at them, and the curtains swayed in a highly distracting fashion. The clock on the mantel-piece grew large and then small in a rhythmic manner, and I began to feel as though the sofa had floated out to sea and we had run into a heavy swell.

Above the rushing noise in my head, I heard Mrs Pringle's boom from the hall.

'I'll tell her, Miss Waters. We'll be glad to see him. She looks very poorly to me – very poorly indeed. Oh, no doubt it'll be hospital with these injuries! Yes, I'll let you know.'

'*I'm not going to hospital!*' I shouted to the open door. Something crashed inside my head and, groaning, I turned my face into the sofa, giving the bump a second wallop.

Mrs Pringle appeared in the doorway.

'It's a good thing it's the first day of the holidays,' she said smugly. 'Give you plenty of time to get over it, won't it, dear?'

I drew in my breath painfully.

'Mrs Pringle,' I said, very quietly and carefully, 'I could do with a little more brandy.'

3 Medical Matters

EXTREME pain, it seems, has a curiously numbing effect on one's normal reactions. Pre-occupied as I was with my afflictions, Mrs Pringle's deplorable remark, which ordinarily would have aroused my fury, now simply appeared to be unhappy but true.

It certainly looked as though a week at least would be needed to put me back into fighting trim. Nursing my arm I began to mourn those blissfully planned picnics, the efficient tidying-up, and the trips to distant places.

'Can't see you doing much in the next week or two,' announced Mrs Pringle, as if divining my melancholy thoughts. 'When my John sprained his ankle at football it was all of three months before he could put his weight on it – and him a *young* man, of course.'

Still cocooned, in my pain, from these barbs, I nodded agreement.

'Tell you what,' said the lady. 'I could come in each morning for an hour or so, seeing as it's holiday time. Get you an egg, say, or some soup to keep you going.'

This was a kind thought and I did my best to register gratitude. By now the arm was beginning to swell, and hurt badly. Would Dr Martin be able to get my sleeve rolled up? Would it have to be cut from the frock?

Alarmed now, I sat up and begged Mrs Pringle to help in my undressing.

'Before the doctor comes?' she asked scandalised.

I explained my fears.

'If that's all, I can slit it up now with the kitchen scissors,' she volunteered, making for the door.

'But I don't want it slit,' I wailed. 'I like this frock! If we can get it off now before this blasted arm gets more and more like a bolster, I can put on my dressing gown.'

'That would look decent enough,' conceded Mrs Pringle, 'and of course I'll stay in the room while he's here. It's only proper.'

She went stumping up the stairs, leaving me to wonder if Dr Martin, now somewhere around seventy, was in any great danger from a plain middle-aged school teacher temporarily one-legged and one-armed.

I could hear Mrs Pringle opening doors above. The room still pitched about, though the swell was not quite as severe as at first.

Closing my eyes, I let myself float gently out to sea upon the sofa.

'Well,' said a man's voice. 'You lost that fight, as far as I can see.'

I opened my eyes and saw Dr Martin surveying me. Mrs Pringle stood beside him.

He pulled up a chair and began to examine the bump on my temple.

'Any pain?'

'Of course there is,' I said, wincing from the pressure of his ice-cold fingers. I explained the symptoms of rocking motions and the movement of furniture in the room.

'Humph!' He felt my skull gently.

'Any pain in the ox-foot?'

'In the *what?*'

'The ox-foot.'

I looked blankly at him.

'The *occiput*, girl,' he explained.

I continued to look at him dumbly.

'The *occiput*, the back of the head, woman!'

'Oh, no, no! None at all,' I assured him. 'Just this bang on the forehead.'

I began to feel rather cross. Why do medical men expect people to know all the Latin terms?

Most patients, I suspect, are as ignorant of anatomy as I am.

My doctor gets a plain statement in basic English from me, and I can't think why his reply cannot be expressed in the same vein.

If I tell him that the bony bump on my wrist hurts, what sort of answer do I get?

It is usually some glib explanation about the action of the lower lobelia on the gloxinia, which may well affect the ageratum and so lead to total tormentilla. Bewildered by all this mumbo-jumbo the patient's normal reaction is to go straight home, apply witch hazel and make a cup of tea.

Dr Martin opened his black bag, moistened some cotton wool and dabbed my forehead.

'You'll survive,' he assured me, as I flinched. He looked across at the brandy bottle.

'Been drinking?'

'Purely for medicinal purposes,' I told him with dignity.

There was a sniff from Mrs Pringle.

'No need to keep you from your work,' said Dr Martin.

Mrs Pringle left the room reluctantly.

'Now, let's look at the arm.'

He felt it and I screamed.

'Can you bend it here?'

'*No!*' I shouted fortissimo. He nodded with evident satisfaction.

'Radial trouble, I think,' he said. 'Have to get it X-rayed.'

At that moment the telephone shrilled, and I heard Mrs Pringle lift the receiver.

By this time, the doctor had produced a calico sling from his bag and was folding it deftly. It smelt horribly of dog biscuits and was very rough when tied round my neck.

'Must keep it still and supported,' he told me. 'You're bound to have a good deal of pain with an elbow injury.'

No one could be kinder than dear Dr Martin, and normally I count him among my most respected friends at Fairacre, but the evident relish with which he imparted this information was hard to bear.

I lay back, exhausted, on the sofa. The pain had frightened me, and I was very careful to keep the arm quite still.

Dr Martin now turned his attention to the ankle. I had taken off my stockings and shoes, and looked morosely at the swelling of my left ankle.

He began to wriggle the toes this way and that, and Mrs Pringle came into the room.

'Mrs Garfield on the phone,' she told us. This was Amy, my old college friend, and it was welcome news. Perhaps she could come to my aid?

'I must speak to her,' I told Dr Martin. 'She might be able to take me into Caxley if I have to go to be X-rayed.'

'Caxley? That's no good to you, my girl. There's no casualty department there now.'

I looked at him in horror.

'Do you mean I've got to be jogged all the way to Norchester?'

'That's right, my dear. And if your friend can take you, the sooner the better.'

The thought of travelling over fifteen miles to our county town appalled me. I lowered my bare legs gingerly to the ground, clutching my wounded arm tenderly the while.

Dr Martin came to my aid, and leaning heavily on his shoulder I hopped to the telephone.

'I've told her you're suffering from an accident,' Mrs Pringle said importantly, as I stood on one foot holding the receiver.

'What's happened?' asked Amy.

I told her.

'I'll be over in half an hour,' she promised. 'Get ready for the hospital and I'll take you straight there.'

My cries of gratitude were cut short by a click and the line going dead.

Amy had gone into action.

By the time she arrived, Dr Martin had departed on his rounds, and I was lying on the sofa, dressed by Mrs Pringle ready for the journey.

It had not been an easy preparation. Fastening stockings to suspenders I now found quite impossible with one hand, and I was obliged to Mrs Pringle for her assistance.

It was equally impossible to put on a coat, and this was draped round my shoulders insecurely. The sling was like emery paper round the back of my neck, until Mrs Pringle managed to insert a silk scarf between it and my scarlet flesh. The ankle had been wrapped in yards of crepe bandage, and I felt as swaddled as an Egyptian mummy.

'You'll be a lot worse before you're better,' Mrs Pringle warned me.

The cupboards had been abandoned since my fall, and I could see she was torn between returning to her duties and tending the fractious sick.

'I'll be all right,' I told her, 'if you like to get on with the work.'

Before she had time to make her decision, the door opened and in walked Amy, looking as elegant as ever in a cream silk suit.

'Poor old love,' she said, in a voice of such warm sympathy, that only Mrs Pringle's presence kept me from shameful weeping.

'What do you need?' she asked more briskly.

'Only this chit from Dr Martin, I think.'

'Then let's ease you into the car and trundle on our way.'

Together, they helped me to hop to Amy's waiting limousine.

'Take the lettuces,' I shouted to Mrs Pringle through the window, 'and your money, and a thousand thanks.'

I finished on a high-pitched yelp as Amy let in the clutch and my elbow moved a millimetre.

'Sorry,' said Amy, looking anxious.

With infinite caution we began our journey.

Amy and I have known each other ever since our college

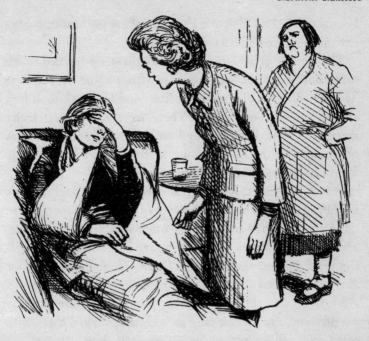

days. She was one of that establishment's brighter stars, excelling in sport as well as work, and would have made a splendid headmistress of some lucky school had she not married within three years of leaving college.

It was quite apparent that James would succeed in anything he took up. He was a dark-eyed charmer, with boundless energy and an effervescent sense of humour. He loved parties and social occasions of all kinds, going to great lengths to arrange outings which would please his friends, and always generous with his time and money.

He was, as the saying goes, 'good with children', and I know it was a blow to both of them that they had no family of their own. Nephews and nieces were frequent visitors to the house, and I think that Amy's spells of supply teaching gave her much-needed contact with children.

These spells grew more frequent as James advanced in his career and was more and more away from home. At this time he was a director of a cosmetic firm, and his work took him abroad several times a year. There were also a great many meetings in the United Kingdom to attend, and Amy was often alone at the lovely house in Bent, the village not far from Caxley and Fairacre, where they lived.

I must confess that I had my suspicions about James's fidelity. He was a warm-hearted gay fellow, as appreciative of pretty women as he was of the other attractive things in life. His frequent absences from home gave him ample opportunities for dalliance, and although I never doubted his love for Amy, some of his absences seemed unusually protracted to me. Added to that, his home-coming presents to Amy were so magnificent, that I personally should have viewed them with some suspicion, even from such a generous man as James.

Amy, however, was completely loyal and discreet. Secretly I had no doubt that she shared my feelings – she was far too astute to be deceived. Nevertheless, nothing had ever been said between us, and our affection increased over the years. Certainly, Amy tends to be bossy, and is always attempting to reform me in one way or another, but I am wonderfully resistant to pressure, as Mrs Pringle knows, and Amy's failure to improve me had not altered the very warm regard which we feel for each other.

This immediate response to my cry for help was typical of her, and I tried to tell her so, as we turned into the hospital grounds.

Still clutching my piece of paper from Dr Martin, I was

ushered into the waiting room of the casualty department, with Amy in attendance.

There were about fifteen of us unfortunates gathered there, some looking, to my inexperienced eye, at the point of death. There were also several children, all of whom appeared to be in excellent spirits.

'Sit down, dear,' said a nurse briskly, pushing up a wheel chair. It struck me smartly behind the knees, so that any modest refusal was cut short as I sat down abruptly.

A lively six-year-old pranced up to make my acquaintance. 'Are you very bad?'

'No,' I said bravely, 'Just my arm and leg are hurt.'

'My sister's bitten her tongue in half,' he said, indicating a screen in the middle distance. 'She won't let them put the stitches in.'

I began to hope that the child would be called away. I had quite enough to bear without all this extra harrowing.

'D'you know what that's for?' he asked, indicating a small scoop about the size of an ash tray, on the arm of my chair.

'No,' I said faintly. Hadn't this horrible child got a mother somewhere?

'It's to be sick in,' he told me.

'Here,' said Amy severely, 'you run away and find a book to read. This lady doesn't want to be bothered with you.'

'I don't want to be bothered with *her* either,' said the horror, moving towards the end of the room, where a battered cardboard box housed a collection of even more battered toys.

He selected a fiendish mechanical car which needed to be run over the tiled floor to make it work. The noise was hideous, but infinitely preferable to the child's company.

He was still at it when I was summoned to be examined by a

37

doctor young enough to be my son. Used as I am to Dr Martin's venerable aspect, I had some qualms, but he was quick and competent and I was despatched to the X-ray department with yet another piece of paper.

Amy waited in the first room and smiled cheerfully at me as I passed to be wheeled down a long corridor. There is nothing, I decided, as we steered an erratic course down the shiny passage, quite so demoralising as being obliged to sit in a push chair.

By now the elbow was torturing me, and no matter how carefully the nurse arranged my arm for the camera I yelped frequently.

'One of the most painful injuries,' she told me, echoing Dr. Martin, 'and of course it can't be put in plaster.'

I heard this with mixed feelings.

'The sling will be a great help,' she assured me, seeing my consternation.

'This one won't,' I told her. 'It's as rough as emery paper.'

'I'll change it,' she promised me. 'This does seem rather antique. Must be war issue.'

She set me up with one rather less scratchy, and I begged her to accept Dr Martin's.

'Dear me, no,' she replied, folding it up briskly. 'Take it home as a spare. After it's been boiled a few times it will be quite comfortable.'

We returned in the push chair to the waiting Amy. The horrible boy had been joined by another, slightly larger, and they were engaged in sticking out their tongues at each other.

'I'm glad you've found a *quieter* game,' said Amy kindly to them.

We waited yet again. At last, my X-ray photographs were displayed on a screen.

'A nasty crack across the radius,' I was told. 'Don't move it for three weeks, and we'll see you then.'

Don't move it, I thought rebelliously! What a hope!

I shuffled crossly towards the door, with Amy in attendance.

'Goodbye, Auntie Hopalong,' shouted the rude boy.

'I think you'd better come straight home with me,' said Amy, as we left the town behind us. 'You can't be alone like this. You're practically helpless, and there are some knock-out pills which I see Dr Martin left on the mantel-piece which you are supposed to take before you go to bed. Lord knows what they'll do!'

'It's terribly good of you, Amy, but I really can't be such a nuisance to you. Besides there are all sorts of things to see to. Tibby, for instance, and the laundry hasn't been sorted, and the groceries arrive tomorrow, and I'll have to make some plans with Mrs Pringle.'

'Then I'll come and stay with you tonight,' said Amy firmly. 'James is away. There's nothing to worry about, and you're certainly not staying alone in the house. So, no arguing.'

I was deeply grateful. If only I could go to sleep, I felt that I would face anything when I woke up. Now all that I craved for was oblivion, and no doubt Dr Martin's pills would help there.

The journey seemed endless, but at last the school house was in sight. I edged my way painfully from the car, and was glad to gain the sitting room.

'Good heavens,' I said, catching sight of the clock. 'It's only half past two! I feel as if I'd been away for a fortnight.'

'I'm going to heat some soup,' said Amy, 'then make up a

bed for you on the couch here. Mrs Pringle's left you a note.'

She handed it to me and then vanished towards the kitchen.

It said:

'Have put all to rights and fed cat. Will come up this evening. Can live in if needed.'

Amy reappeared in the doorway.

'I take back all I've ever said about Mrs Pringle,' I told her, giving her the note to read.

'A handsome offer,' agreed Amy.

'Downright noble,' I said warmly.

'And how long,' said Amy, 'do you think you two could rub along together?'

'Well –' I began, and was cut short by Amy's laughter.

4 Amy Takes Command

THOSE of us who are lucky enough to live in a village, face the fact that our lives are an open book. Those dreadful stories of town-dwellers found dead in their beds, having been there for months, and even years sometimes, are not likely to be echoed in smaller communities.

Here, in Fairacre, villagers tardy in bringing in their milk bottles run the risk of well-meaning neighbours popping round 'to see if they are all right.'

There are times when this concern for each other seems downright irritating. On the other hand, how comforting it is to know that people care about one's welfare!

Mrs Pringle, of course, had not been able to resist telling several of her friends about the drama in which she had taken part that morning.

Thanks to one of Dr Martin's pills I knew nothing from three o'clock that afternoon until I woke at ten that night, but Amy evidently had a succession of visitors during that time, and was very touched by their sympathy and their practical offers of help.

'The vicar's wife brought those roses,' she told me, waving towards a mixed bouquet which smelt heavenly on the bedside table.

'And she says you are not to worry about the organ on Sunday, as she is quite able to cope if she transposes everything into the key of C, and they cut out the anthem.'

I clutched my aching head with my sound hand.

'I'd forgotten all about that!'

'Well, keep on forgetting,' Amy advised me. 'You'll have to get used to the brutal fact that no one is indispensable.'

I nodded meekly, and wished I hadn't. Those pills were dynamite.

'And Mrs Willet's sent six gorgeous eggs and some tomatoes, and will do any washing while your arm's useless.'

'That woman's an angel. Luckily, her husband recognises it.'

'Someone from the farm – I didn't catch the name –'

'Mrs Roberts.'

'That's it. She'll help in any way you like. Shopping, bringing you a midday meal. Anything!'

'People *are* kind.'

'They most certainly are,' agreed Amy, 'and I am absolutely flabbergasted at the way they're all rallying round you.'

I felt slightly nettled. Anyone would think that I am normally such a monster that I do not deserve any consideration. I was deeply grateful for all this concern, but Amy's astonishment was hard to bear.

'It isn't as though they have children at the school,' went on Amy, musing to herself.

'Even Mrs Pringle,' she continued thoughtfully, 'called this evening to see how you were.'

She sighed, then jumped up to straighten the counterpane.

'Ah well! People are odd,' she said, dismissing the subject.

But by this time, my irritation was waning, for Dr Martin's blue pill was wafting me once more into oblivion.

* * *

The sun was warm upon the bed when I awoke. It shone through the petals of the roses, and sent their fragrance through the room.

Amy was gazing at me anxiously.

'Thank God, you've woken up! I was beginning to wonder if you'd ever come to.'

'Why, what's the time?'

'Ten o'clock.'

'No! I must have had about sixteen hours' sleep.'

'How do you feel?'

'Marvellous, if I don't move.'

'Could you manage an egg?'

I sat up cautiously.

'I could manage an egg and toast and marmalade and butter and lashings of coffee and perhaps an apple.'

Amy laughed.

'You've recovered. Do you ever lose your appetite?'

'It improves in a crisis,' I assured her. 'When war broke out, I ate with enormous gusto. The more sensitive types on the staff of that school I was at then, couldn't touch a morsel – or so they said – but I had the feeling each meal might be my last, so I made the most of it.'

Amy laughed, and went to the kitchen.

I could hear her moving china and saucepans, and lay back feeling one part guilty and nine parts relieved. How pleasant it was to be waited on! I tried to remember the last time I had lain in bed while someone else cooked my breakfast, and found it beyond my powers.

Tibby came undulating into the room giving little chirrups of pleasure at having found me at last. She jumped elegantly on to the bed, missing my damaged ankle by a millimetre. I clasped my poor arm in trepidation. Tibby's affectionate attention was a mixed blessing this morning.

Before she could do much damage, Amy appeared with the tray.

'I've cut your toast into fingers, my dear, and I'll spread your marmalade when you want it.'

'I feel about three years old,' I told her, 'and backward at that.'

Eating a boiled egg left-handed is no easy task, and I should certainly have gone without butter and marmalade if Amy had not been there to help me. Suddenly, I realised how horribly helpless I was. It was frightening.

'Now, about plans,' said Amy, putting down the knife.

'With all these offers of help from kind neighbours, I should be fine,' I said.

She looked at me quizzically.

'You haven't tried walking yet, or washing, or doing your hair or dressing.'

'No,' I agreed sadly.

'And let's face it, you can't possibly negotiate the stairs even with that ankle strapped.'

I knew this was the plain truth.

'I've thought it all out. You're coming back to Bent with me. There's plenty of room. I shall be glad of your company, and it will do you good to have a change of scene. So say no more.'

'It's more than generous of you, Amy, but – '

'It's no use arguing. I know what you are going to say. Well, Tibby can come too, or Mrs Pringle has offered to come in to feed her, so that's that. We can shut up the house and give Mrs P. the key. Mr Willet says he'll keep an eye on the garden and mow the grass.'

'But Dr Martin . . . ?'

'Dr Martin can be kept informed of your progress by telephone, and is welcome to visit you at my house.'

I looked at Amy with admiration.

'You've worked it all out to the last detail, I see.'

'I had plenty of time yesterday – and lots of offers from others, don't forget.'

I nodded in silence.

'Let's get you along to the bath.'

Bracing my arm stiffly, for I dreaded the pain when it was moved, I struggled to get my legs to the floor. Once they were there it was obvious that only the right one could bear any weight. Amy was quite right, I was helpless.

She was looking at me with some amusement.

'Well?'

'You win, you lovely girl. I'll come thankfully, bless you.'

One arm round her shoulders, I shimmied my way to the bathroom.

We were seen off that afternoon by a number of friends and well-wishers. I began to feel rather a fraud. After all, no one could say I was seriously ill.

Nevertheless, it was delightful to receive as much sympathy and attention.

'The vicar and I will visit you next week,' promised Mrs Partridge.

'I've taken the dirty clothes,' called Mrs Willet.

'And I'll give the place a proper bottoming, cupboards and

all, before you're back,' said Mrs Pringle, in a tone which sounded more like a threat than a promise.

We moved off, waving like royalty, to the accompaniment of Tibby's yowling from a cat-basket borrowed from Mr Roberts.

It is only about half an hour's run to Bent but I was mightily glad to arrive at Amy's house and to be ensconced in the spare room. Some wise person in the past had made sure that the window sills in the bedroom were low enough for the bed-ridden to admire the view, for which I was truly grateful.

Beyond Amy's immaculate garden, bright with lilies and roses, stretched rolling agricultural land. The crops were already ripening, and no doubt the combines would be out in the fields long before my beastly arm was fit to use. In the middle distance, a blue tractor trundled between the hedges on its way to the fields, and near at hand, on Amy's bird table, tits and starlings squabbled over food.

There would be plenty here to amuse me. How good Amy was! She had made light of taking me on, useless as I was, but I knew how much extra work I should be making, and determined to get downstairs as soon as possible.

Tibby, released from the hated basket, was roaming cautiously about the room, sniffing at Amy's rose and cream decor with the greatest suspicion and dislike. She had deigned to drink a little milk, but was clearly going to take some time to settle down.

'You are an ungrateful cat,' I told her. 'You might well have been left behind with Mrs Pringle, and she would have bottomed you with the rest of the house.'

Amy entered with the tea tray.

'I imagine heaven's like this,' I said. 'Perfect surroundings, and angels wafting in with the tea.'

'But this one's going to watch you spread your own jam this time,' she warned me.

Later that evening, as the summer dusk fell and the scent of the lime flowers hung heavy on the air, Amy sat by the lamp and stitched away at her tapestry. A moth fluttered round the light, tapping a staccato tattoo on the shade, but Amy did not seem aware of it.

It was very quiet in the room. It seemed to me that Amy was unusually pensive, and although she had enough to think of,

47

in all conscience, with me on her hands, somehow I felt her thoughts were elsewhere.

'Amy,' I began, 'you know I can't thank you enough for all you're doing, but won't I be even more of a burden when James comes home?'

'It won't be for several days,' said Amy, snipping a thread. 'It may be even longer. There was some possibility of going straight on to Scotland, if he can arrange things with somebody at the office to attend to that end and save him coming back again.'

There was something in Amy's tone which disquieted me. Despondency? Resignation? Hopelessness?

I had never seen Amy in this mood, and wondered what was the cause.

'I don't think I shall need a blue pill tonight,' I said, changing the subject. 'I can hardly keep awake as it is.'

'I'm horribly sleepy too,' confessed Amy. She began to roll up her work, and glanced at the clock.

'James usually rings about eight, but something must have stopped him. No doubt there will be a letter in the post in the morning. I shan't wait up any longer.'

She rose, and came close to the bed.

'Have you got all you need? I've left this little bell to ring if you need me in the night, and I shall prop my door ajar. Tibby's settled in the kitchen, so there's nothing for you to worry about.'

She bent to give me a rare kiss on the forehead.

'Sleep well. I'll see you in the morning.'

After Amy had gone, I turned out the light and slid carefully down the bed. Tired though I was, I could not sleep.

It grieved me to see Amy so unhappy. Something more than my problems was eating at her heart. I had not known Amy for over thirty years without being able to measure her moods.

That James was at the bottom of it all, I had no doubt. Was the rapscallion more than usually entangled this time? Was their marriage seriously threatened by the present philanderings?

It is at times like this that a spinster counts her blessings. Her troubles are of her own making, and can be tackled straightforwardly. She is independent, both monetarily and in spirit. Her life is wonderfully simple, compared with that of her married sister. And she cannot be hurt, quite so cruelly, as a woman can be by her husband.

Conversely, she has no-one with whom to share her troubles and doubts. She must bear alone the consequences of all her actions and, coming down to brass tacks, she must be able to support herself financially, physically and emotionally.

I know all this from first-hand experience. I know too that there are some people who view my life as narrow and self-centred. Some, even, find a middle-aged single woman pitiable, if not faintly ridiculous. This, I have always felt, is to rate the value of men too highly, although I recognise that a truly happy marriage is probably the highest state of contentment attainable by either partner.

But how often something mars the partnership! Jealousy, indolence, illness, family difficulties, money troubles – so much can go wrong when two lives are joined.

Outside, in the darkness, a screech owl gave its blood-curdling cry. A shadow crept over the moon, and turning my face into the comfort of a pillow – supplied by James – I decided that it was time for sleep.

5 Recovery at Bent

THE days passed very agreeably at Amy's. Time hangs heavily, some people say, when there is nothing to do, but I found, in my enforced idleness, that the hours flew by.

The weather had changed from its earlier brilliance. The sky was overcast, the air was still. There was something curiously restful about these soft grey days. The air was mild and I sat in the garden a great deal, nursing my arm and propping my battered ankle on a foot-rest.

Amy had a small pond with a tinkling fountain in her garden, and the sound of the splashing water was often the only noise to be heard. I felt stronger daily, and began to get very clever at using my left hand. I was more and more conscious how much I owed to Amy's generosity of spirit. Without her care and companionship these early days of progress would have been much slower.

During these quiet days I had the opportunity of observing Amy as she went about her tasks. She dealt with her domestic routine with great efficiency, and I began to realise, at the end of a week, that without the method with which she approached each chore, I should have been alone far more often. As it was, she had time to sit and talk to me, or simply to sit beside me and read, or work at her tapestry. I think we grew closer together, in those few days, than we had ever been before.

Very little mention was made of James, although Amy did say one evening that he had telephoned to say that he was in Scotland and would not be returning for a week or so. The determinedly gay manner in which she told me this, confirmed my fears that Amy herself was a very worried woman. It made her kindness to me doubly dear.

One morning I was taking my cautious walk in the garden, leaning heavily upon a fine ebony stick of James's, when I was horrified to see the corpse of a hedgehog floating in the pond. Obviously, it had tried to reach the water, toppled in, and been unable to scramble out again. It was a pathetic sight, and I was wondering how I could get it out when Amy called from the house, and emerged with one of her friends, Gerard Baker.

I had met him first at one of Amy's parties, and several times since then. He had been collecting material for a book about minor Victorian poets, and visited Fairacre once or twice to learn more about our one poet Aloysius Stone.

We, in Fairacre, are rather proud of Aloysius, who lived in one of the cottages in Tyler's Row, and was somewhat of a trial at village concerts in the early part of the century. He loved the opportunity of reciting his poems, and was apt to go on for far longer than his allotted time, much to the consternation of the programme organisers and the out-spokenness of his audience.

'This is a great day,' said Amy after we had exchanged greetings, and Gerard had commiserated with me about my battered condition. She held up a book.

'Not *The Book*?' I said.

'The very same,' said Gerard. 'Came out last month.'

'Well! And I didn't hear a thing.'

'I'm not surprised. I shouldn't think a book ever crept out into the world with as little notice as this one had.'

'But surely it will be reviewed? After all your hard work you're bound to have some recognition.'

'I doubt it. I'm not carping. There aren't exactly queues at the bookshop doors for *any* book, and one about Victorian poets won't set the Thames on fire. If it covers the costs I'll be content, and so will the publishers.'

By this time, Amy had walked across to the pond, and was studying the floating corpse with some distaste.

'Give me a rake,' said Gerard, approaching, 'and I'll fish the poor thing out for you.'

We surveyed the pathetic body, the shiny black snout, the brindled prickles, the scaly black legs.

Amy returned with the rake.

'It's really dead, I suppose?' she asked, bending closer to examine the corpse.

'Well, I can tell you flat,' said Gerard, casting his rake, 'that I'm not volunteering to give it the kiss of life! There are limits to the milk of human kindness.'

He fished the body to the edge and lifted it out.

'I think a distant patch of nettles, or some such rough cover, would be his best shroud. You aren't proposing burial? I'm no great shakes with a spade.'

'Good heavens, no, Gerard dear!' exclaimed Amy. 'Follow me, and we'll put him over the hedge into the ditch in the cornfield, poor little sweet.'

' "Sweet" ', said Gerard, his nose wrinkled, 'is not quite the word for it.'

He followed Amy towards the end of the garden, balancing the dripping victim precariously on the rake. I watched the funeral cortege from my chair with some amusement. The more I saw of Gerard Baker, the more I liked him.

He was clever but unaffected, sympathetic but not mawkish, and had a cheerful practical approach to problems – such as this present one – which I found wholly admirable. No wonder Amy welcomed him.

'What about a restorative?' she said when they returned. 'Gin, sherry?'

'Could it be coffee?' asked Gerard.

'Of course.' She went into the house.

'What a marvel she is!' exclaimed Gerard.

'I'll endorse that,' I said, and told him how wonderfully she had coped with me.

'Typical,' said Gerard. 'I was full of admiration for the way in which she coped with that lovelorn niece of hers, Vanessa.'

'I believe we may see something of her before long,' I told him. 'Evidently she's quite got over that infatuation. You know she's in Scotland? Working in a hotel?'

Gerard, to my surprise, looked somewhat embarrassed.

'Yes, I did know. As a matter of fact, I happened to call at the hotel a week or two ago. She seemed in great spirits.'

'Did you hear that, Amy?' I cried, as she put down the tray. 'Gerard has seen Vanessa, and she's very well.'

Amy shot a lightning glance at Gerard's face, and looked away quickly. He was endeavouring to look nonchalant, and not succeeding very well.

'I was in the district. I'm collecting material for a book about Scottish poets – a companion volume to the Victorian one, I hope, – and I remembered the name of the hotel.'

'How nice! Is she flourishing?'

'In very good spirits. She said something about a holiday soon, and I gather she may come and see you.'

'That's right,' agreed Amy. She poured the coffee.

'Any news of the young Scotsman who was being so attentive?' she asked. Her tone was polite, but I detected a hint of mischief in her face.

Gerard had recovered his composure.

'I didn't hear anything about him. No doubt there are a number of attentive young Scotsmen. Vanessa's looking very attractive these days. Quite a change of aspect from the time when she was mourning the Chilean.'

'Bolivian!' said Amy and I together.

We sipped our coffee, relaxed and happy. A red admiral butterfly flitted decoratively from flower to flower in the herbaceous border, and I remember the pale unhappy Vanessa whose passion for a four-times-married foreigner had blinded her to all summer delights on the first occasion of our meeting. She had spent a week with Amy then, and I don't think I had ever seen my normally resilient friend quite so exhausted.

'And how's Fairacre?' enquired Gerard. 'What of my friend Mr Willet?'

I gave him a brief account of village affairs to date, and conversation grew general. It was half-past eleven before he leapt to his feet, protesting that he must be off.

'I've an aunt living not far from here, and I'm taking her out to lunch. She's eighty-five and a demon for exercise. Think of me at about two-thirty, walking my legs off along some cart track.'

'Come again,' said Amy.

'I will,' he promised. 'But no corpses next time, please.'

*　　　*　　　*

That afternoon I broached the subject of my return home to Amy. I had been with her for well over a week, looked after as never before, and felt that I really could not impose upon her much longer.

'But I love to have you,' she assured me.

'You're too kind. There are lots of things you must be neglecting, and surely there's a holiday cropping up soon?'

I remember that she had discussed a visit to Crete earlier in the year. Nothing had been said about it while I had been staying at Bent, and it occurred to me that perhaps the plans had fallen through.

'That's nearly a fortnight away,' said Amy.

'You'll probably need to go shopping.'

'That doesn't mean that you've got to go back to Fairacre.'

I pointed out that there were a number of matters to attend to at home. There were some school forms to be filled up, and a certain amount of organisation for next term. My domestic arrangements also needed some attention, though no doubt Mrs Pringle's bottoming would be almost finished.

'I'm mobile now,' I said, stretching out my lumpy ankle. 'Why, I can even dress myself if I keep to button-down-the-front things, and remember to thread the bad arm through the sleeve first!'

'You're getting above yourself,' Amy smiled. 'I really think you *are* getting better.'

She surveyed me with her head on one side.

'I can see you're really bent on going. Tell you what. Let's drive over tomorrow afternoon and get the place ready, and see if you can manage the stairs and so on. If so, I'll install you the day after.'

And so it was agreed.

Amy took up her tapestry and I turned the pages of a magazine.

The thought of going home excited me. I should never cease to be grateful to my old friend, but I longed to potter about my own home, to get back to my books and my garden, to see the familiar birds on the bird table, and to smell the pinks in my border again. Tibby, too, would welcome the return.

Beyond Amy's window the rain was falling. Grey veils drifted across the fields, blotting the distant hills from view. It made the drawing-room seem doubly snug.

'I wonder how long it will be before I can do without this confounded sling,' I mused aloud. 'I can wriggle my fingers quite well. How long does a bone take to mend?'

Amy looked at me thoughtfully.

'Weeks at our age, I imagine.'

'I'm not decrepit, and I don't feel old.'

'I do now and again,' said Amy, with a vigour that belied her words. 'I find myself behaving like an old lady sometimes. You know, never walking up escalators, and not minding if young things like Vanessa stand up when I enter a room.'

'I haven't got quite to that stage yet.'

'But when I start pinning brooches on my hats,' said Amy, resuming her stitching, 'I shall know I'm *really* old.'

There was a companionable silence for a while. Outside, the rain grew heavier, and began to patter at the windows.

'Of course, I think about dying now and again,' I said.

'Who doesn't?'

'What do you do about it?'

'Well,' said Amy, snipping a thread, 'I make sure I'm wearing respectable corsets – not my comfortable ones with the elastic stretched and speckled with rubber bits – and I pay up outstanding bills and, frankly, there's not much else one can do, is there, dear?'

'But hope,' I finished for her.

'But hope,' she echoed.

She turned her gaze upon the rain-swept view through the window. There had been a dying fall in those last two words.

It was plain that it was the sadness of living, not of dying, which preoccupied my friend's thoughts.

And my heart grieved for her.

The next afternoon we drove from Bent to Fairacre. The rain had ceased, leaving everything fresh and fragrant. The sun shone, striking rainbows from the droplets on the hedge, and in its summer strength drawing steam from the damp roads. Sprays of wild roses arched towards the ground, weighted with the water which trembled in their shell-pink cups, and everywhere the scent of honeysuckle hung upon the air.

In the lush fields the cattle steamed as they fed, and birds splashed joyously in their wayside baths. Everywhere one looked there was rejoicing in the sunshine after the rain, and my spirits rose accordingly.

As Fairacre drew nearer I grew happier and happier, until I broke into singing.

Amy began to laugh.

'What an incorrigible home-bird you are! You remind me of Timmy Willie.'

'When he was asked what he did when it rained in the country?' I enquired.

' "When it rains",' quoted Amy, dodging a fat thrush in the road, ' "I sit in my little sandy burrow and shell corn and seeds".'

' "And when the sun comes out again," ' I finished for her,

' "You should see my garden and the flowers – roses and pinks and pansies." '

'I'm sorry for children who aren't brought up on Beatrix Potter,' said Amy. 'Look! There's St Patrick's spire ahead. You'll be back in your burrow in two shakes.'

The lane to the school was empty, and we arrived unseen by the neighbours. It was very quiet, the village sunk in the somnolence of early afternoon.

Inside the school house everything was unusually tidy. A few fallen petals from the geranium on the window sill made it look more like home, however, counteracting the symmetrically draped tea-cloths on the airer, and the 'Vim', washing up liquid and so on, which were arrayed with military precision in order of height on the draining board. Every polished surface winked with cleanliness. Never had the stove flashed so magnificently. Never had the windows been so clear. Even the doormat looked as if it had been brushed and combed.

'Well,' said Amy, gazing round. 'Mrs Pringle's had a field day here.'

Awe-struck, we went into the sitting room. Here, the same unnatural tidiness was apparent.

'I feel as though I ought to take off my shoes,' I said. 'It's positively holy with cleanliness.'

The coffee pot on the dresser, behind which I stuff all the letters needing an answer, now stood at the extreme side of the board. There was nothing – not even a single sheet of paper – behind it.

'Save us!' I cried. 'Where on earth is all my correspondence?'

'Gone to heaven on a bonfire,' Amy replied.

'But I *must* have it,' I began in bewilderment.

'Calm down,' said Amy, 'or you'll break your arm again.'

This idiotic remark had the effect of calming us both. We sat down, somewhat nervously, on the newly washed chair covers.

'She's washed every blessed thing in sight,' I said wonderingly, 'and I declare she's oiled the beams too. Look at the fire-irons! And the candlesticks! And the lamp shades! It's positively uncanny. I shall never be able to live up to this standard.'

'Don't worry,' said Amy comfortingly. 'By the time you've had twenty-four hours here, it will look as though a tornado has hit it, and it will be just like home again.'

It was one of those remarks which could have been more delicately expressed, or, better still, been left unsaid. In normal circumstances I might have made some sharp retort, but Amy's kindness over the past week or so enabled me to hold my tongue.

We sat for a few minutes, resting and marvelling at Mrs Pringle's handiwork before embarking on a tour of the whole house. It was a relief to find that I could negotiate the stairs if I attacked them like a toddler, bringing both feet to one stair before essaying the next. I could have wished the banister had been placed on the left hand side instead of the right, but by assuming a crab-like motion I could get up and down very well and was suitably smug about it.

'And what about getting in and out of the bath?' asked Amy, deflating me.

'I'm going to get one of those rubber mats, so that I don't slip,' I told her. 'And I shall *kneel* down to bath, so that I can get up again easily.'

Amy laughed.

'You win, my love. If the worst comes to the worst, you can

always ring me, and I'll nip over and scrub your back.'

We checked the goods in the larder, and made out a shopping list, and then went to inspect the garden. As well as Timmy Willie's roses and pinks and pansies, the purple clematis had come out, the velvety flowers glorious against the old bricks of the house.

We sat together on the rustic seat warmed by the sun, and tilted up our faces to the blaze as thankfully as the daisies on the grass.

Tomorrow, I thought, I shall be back for good. As if reading my thoughts, Amy spoke.

'No place like home, eh?'

She sounded relaxed and slightly amused at my happiness.

'None,' I said fervently.

6 Amy Needs Help

I WOKE next morning in jubilant spirits. Through the bedroom window I could see two men examining the standing corn. No doubt the farmer was hoping to start cutting later in the day when the dew had vanished. I should not be there to see it, I thought happily.

The harvest fields of Bent would be far distant. I should be watching Mr Roberts, our local farmer, trundling the combine round our Fairacre fields. But that would be a week or so later, for our uplands are colder than the southward slopes of Amy's countryside, and all our crops are a little later.

Amy and I lingered over our coffee cups. I was looking hopefully among the newspaper columns for some crumb of cheer among the warfare, murders, rapes and attacks upon old men and women for any small change they might have had upon them, without – as usual – much success. Amy was busy with her letters.

She had left until last a bulky envelope addressed in James's unmistakable hand. She slit it open, her face grave, and gave the pages her close attention. I refilled her coffee cup and my own, in the silence, and turned to an absorbing account of a woman with nine children and a tenth on the way, who had struck her husband over the head with a handy frying pan, after some little difference about methods of birth control.

She was reported as saying that 'he didn't like interfering

with Nature,' and I was glad to see that her solicitor was putting up a spirited defence. I wished her luck. Really, marriage was no bed of roses for some women, I thought, congratulating myself, yet again, on my single state.

The rustling of paper brought me back to the present. Amy was stuffing the letter back into the envelope. Her mouth was set grimly, and I looked hastily at the newspaper again.

I was conscious that Amy was staring blindly across the cornfields. I finished my coffee and rose.

'If you'll excuse me,' I said, 'I'll go and finish packing.'

There was no reply from Amy. Still as a statue, she stared stonily before her, as I crept away.

An hour or so later, we packed up the car together. Amy seemed to have recovered her good humour, and we laughed about the amount of luggage I seemed to have accumulated.

Tibby's basket took up a goodly part of the back seat. An old mackintosh had been folded and placed strategically beneath it. We had had trouble before, and were determined to prevent Amy's lovely car 'smelling like a civet's paradise', to quote Mr Willet, referring to the poet Aloysius Stone's noisome house long ago.

Two cases, a pile of books, a bulky dressing gown and a basket of vegetables and flowers from Amy's garden, filled the rest of the back seat and the boot, and we still had a box of groceries to collect from Bent's village stores.

'Anyone would think we were off for a fortnight's holiday,' observed Amy, surveying the luggage.

'Well, you will be soon,' I said.

Amy's smile vanished, and I cursed myself for clumsiness.

'Let's hope so,' she said soberly.

I edged myself into the passenger seat while Amy returned to the house to lock up. How I wished I could help her! She had been so good to me, so completely selfless and welcoming, that it was doubly hard to see her unhappy.

But nothing could be done if she preferred to keep her troubles to herself. I respected her reticence. Too often I have been the unwilling recipient of confidences, knowing full well that, later, the impulsive babbler would regret her disclosures as much as I regretted hearing them. 'Least said, soonest mended', is an old adage which reflects much wisdom. I could only admire Amy's stoicism, and hope that one day, somehow, I should be able to help her.

We set off for Fairacre, stopping only once to pick up the groceries. Our pace was sedate, for the faster we went the shriller grew Tibby's wails of protest from the wicker basket. Even at thirty-five miles an hour the noise was ear-splitting.

'I meant to have told you,' shouted Amy above the racket, 'that I had a letter from Vanessa this morning. She's coming down for a day next week. She's on holiday, I gather.'

'Bring her over if she can spare the time,' I shouted back.

Amy nodded.

'Funny thing about Gerard, wasn't it?' she said at last. 'Do you smell a romance?'

'What? Between Gerard and Vanessa?'

'Yes. I thought he looked remarkably like a cat that has got at the cream when he spoke of her.'

I digested this unwillingly.

'No, I don't think so,' I said finally. 'He's years older.'

'A mature man,' began Amy, in what I recognised as her experienced-woman-of-the-world voice, 'is often *exactly* what a young thing like Vanessa *needs*. She probably knows this subconsciously. She's very intelligent really underneath all that dreadful clothing and flowing hair. I shall do my best to encourage it.'

I began to feel alarmed for both innocent parties. Amy, on match-making bent, has a flinty ruthlessness, as I know to my cost. On this occasion, however, I decided to keep silent.

An ominous pattering sound, as of water upon newspaper, distracted our attention from Vanessa and Gerard, and directed it upon Tibby.

'Thank God for the mackintosh!' exclaimed Amy, accelerating slightly.

We drew up with a flourish at the school house, and let the cat escape into the kitchen, where she stalked about, sniffing at the unusual cleanliness with much the same expression of amazement which Amy and I had worn.

We unpacked, and Amy insisted on putting a hot water bottle into my bed, despite the bright sunshine. We made coffee, and I asked Amy to stay to lunch.

'Scrambled egg,' I said. 'I can whip up eggs with my left hand beautifully.'

'I mustn't, my dear,' she said rising. 'James comes home tonight, and there's a lot to do.'

'Then I won't keep you,' I said, and went on to try and thank her once again for all she had done. She brushed my efforts aside.

'It was good to have company,' she said.

'Well, you'll have James now.'

'Only for a day or so. We've a lot to discuss before the holiday. Some of it, I fear, not very agreeable.'

She climbed into the car and waved goodbye, leaving me to savour her last sentence.

It was, I discovered later, the biggest understatement of Amy's life.

During the afternoon, Mrs Pringle called.

I invited her in, and thanked her from my heart for all she had done.

'The house,' I told her, 'is absolutely transfigured. You must have spent hours here.'

A rare smile curved Mrs Pringle's lips. Her mouth normally turns down, giving her a somewhat reptilian look. Turned upwards, it had the strange effect as if a frog had smiled.

'Well, it needed it,' said Mrs Pringle. 'What I found in them chair covers when I pulled them out is nobody's business. Pencils, knitting needles, nuts, bits of paper, and there was even a boiled sweet.'

'No!' I cried. 'What, all sticky?'

Slattern though I am, I could not believe that a sucked sweet would turn up in the debris.

'Luckily it was wrapped in a bit of cellophane,' conceded Mrs Pringle. 'But it is not what anyone'd have found when Mrs Hope was here.'

'Have a cup of tea?' I asked, changing the subject abruptly. Mrs Hope's example leads to dangerous ground. Over the tea cups, Mrs Pringle brought me up to date with village news. The Scouts were having a mammoth jumble sale. (All our village jumble sales are 'mammoth'). The Caxley bus was now an hour earlier on market day, and a dratted nuisance everybody found it. The new people at Tyler's Row had bought a puppy, and Mr Mawne had seen a pair of waxworks in the garden.

I must admit that this last snippet of news took me aback,

65

until I remembered that Henry Mawne's hobby is ornithology and Mrs Pringle was probably referring to waxwings.

'I thought they came in the winter,' I hazarded.

'Maybe they do,' agreed Mrs Pringle. 'But that garden of the Mawnes is always perishing cold. It may have confused the waxworks.'

Privately, I thought that they were not the only ones to be confused, and we let the matter drop.

'While your arm's mending,' said Mrs Pringle, 'I'll be in each morning for an hour.' I thanked her.

She rose to go, looking with pride at the tidiness around her.

'Don't want to see this slide back into the usual mess,' she said, echoing Amy, and departed.

The next two or three days passed pleasurably, and I gloried in my growing accomplishments. I found that I could lift my right arm, if I held it at exactly the correct angle, and even began to comb the hair on my *occiput* with my right hand. I became quite nimble at mounting and descending the stairs, and each small triumph cheered me greatly.

One morning Amy rang me.

'Vanessa is with me. May we come over?'

I expressed my delight.

'And another thing,' said Amy, and stopped.

'Yes?'

'Perhaps I should wait until I see you.'

It was most unlike Amy to shilly-shally like this.

'What's it about?'

'Crete.'

'Crete? I don't know a thing about it! Do you want to borrow a map or something?'

'No. I want you to consider visiting it with me, as my guest, of course.'

I was struck dumb.

'Are you still there?'

'Partially.'

'Well, think about it. James can't come, but wants me to go ahead with the holiday. We'll talk about it later.'

There was a click and the line went dead.

Dazed by this thunderbolt, I wandered vaguely through the open French window, caught my poor arm on the latch and, cursing, returned to earth again.

The two arrived soon after lunch, and in the meantime I had turned over this truly wonderful invitation in my mind. Of course, I should love to go, and so much better was I, that my disabilities would not hold up proceedings in any way. We should be back several days before term began. Mrs Pringle, no doubt, would be only too glad to have charge of the house again, and the local kennels would look after Tibby—not, of course, to the cat's complete satisfaction—but perfectly well.

On the other hand, I had accepted so much from Amy already that I hardly liked to take an expensive holiday as well. My bank balance would certainly not stand the expense of paying my share, which would be the right thing to do, and so I felt that I really should refuse, sad though it was.

It was good to see Vanessa again. She was dressed in a white trouser suit with a scarlet blouse, unbuttoned to the waist, under which she wore nothing. I was rather perplexed about this. Did she know that she was unbuttoned? Should she be told? I decided to say nothing, but felt rather relieved that no men were in the party.

On her feet were two bright red shoes, so clumsy and stub-toed that they might have been football boots, and in her hand was a minute bag of silver mesh of the kind that my grandmother carried at evening parties.

But her long hair was as lustrous as ever, and her looks much improved since the overthrow of the Bolivian Roderick who had so fascinated the poor child when last she was in Fairacre.

On her first visit to the school house she had said practically nothing. Today she rattled on, with much animation, about Scotland and her work at the hotel.

'And you saw Gerard?' I could not resist saying.

Her face lit up.

'Wasn't it lucky? He happened to be nearby. I can't tell you how lovely it was to see him again. We write sometimes, but it's not the same thing as meeting.'

She clapped a hand to her brow, and looked anxiously at Amy. 'The book! Did we bring it?'

'In the car,' said Amy. 'It's for Mr Willet,' she explained. 'Gerard asked Vanessa if she would deliver it as he knew we were coming to Fairacre.'

'I'll walk down,' said Vanessa, scrambling to her feet. She surveyed the red football boots proudly. 'These are real walking shoes, the girl in the shop told me. But, of course, I mustn't get them wet.'

'Why not?' I asked. 'Surely shoes are worn for the purpose of keeping the feet dry.'

'Not these days,' Vanessa assured me pityingly. 'That's a very old-fashioned idea. Today the shoes have a label on saying that they mustn't be used in the wet.'

She smiled upon me kindly, and went off for the book.

Now that we were alone, Amy turned directly to the

68

subject which was uppermost in our minds.

'Well? What do you think? Would you like to see Crete?'

'I'd love to –,' I began.

'It won't be quite as lovely as it was when I first saw it one April. It's bound to be drier and hotter, but the air in the mountains is delicious, and there is plenty of shade at the hotel.'

'But, Amy,' I persisted. 'I really can't accept a holiday like this.'

'Why not, for heaven's sake? It's all paid for and arranged. You'd simply be taking over the plane seat and James's bed and board. Perfectly straightforward.'

'But I can't afford it, my dear.'

'No one wants you to afford it. I told you that, so put that out of your dear, upright, puritanical mind. I should be most grateful for your company. It would be a kindness from *you* to *me*. Not the other way round.'

'You've done so much already,' I said, weakening.

'Right,' said Amy briskly. 'Return the compliment, and help me out.'

She jumped up suddenly and went to the window. Her back towards me, she spoke quickly.

'Things are very rough between James and me at the moment. I'm quite used to seeing him make a minor ass of himself over a pretty face, now and again, but this time I'm frightened. He's deadly serious about some young thing about Vanessa's age. I've never seen him so determined, so ruthless –.'

Her voice broke, and I moved swiftly to comfort her. She shook her head violently.

'Don't be kind to me, or sympathise, or I shall sob my heart out, and have eyes like red gooseberries.'

She fought for control, and then continued.

'He wants me to give him a divorce. I've refused to consider such a step, until we've both had time to think things over. We shall stay apart for a few weeks, and he wants me to go to Crete as arranged and have a break. Apart from this terrifying singleness of purpose about the girl, he's as considerate as ever. It makes it all the more incredible.'

She turned to face me. Her poor face was crumpled and her eyes were wet.

'Now will you come with me?' she pleaded.

'Yes, please,' I said, with no more hesitation.

7 Flying Away

FAIRACRE'S reaction to my proposed foreign jaunt was swift and varied.

The first person to be told was Mrs Pringle, of course, when she arrived the next morning to repair any havoc I might have caused overnight. Her response was typical.

'If you ask for my opinion,' she began heavily, (I hadn't, but was obviously going to get it) 'then I should say you was very unwise indeed!'

She folded her arms across her cretonne-clad bosom, and settled down to a good gossip.

'I take it this place is in the Mediterranean?'

I said that it was.

'Then don't touch the fish,' said Mrs Pringle, warming to her subject. 'The pollution out there's something chronic, and the fish don't stand a dog's chance, if you follow me.'

I nodded.

'And keep the water off of that arm of yours – no bathing or any of that lark, or you'll be writhing in agony from *germs*.'

'Oh really – !' I began to expostulate.

'Furthermore,' went on Mrs Pringle ruthlessly, 'lay off the fruit and veg. unless they've been cooked. An aunt of mine had a very nasty rash from eating raw fruit in Malta. Disfiguring, as well as irritating. Never looked the same after, and she had been a nice looking woman when made up.'

I said that I should take all reasonable precautions, and rose, hoping that Mrs Pringle would take the hint.

'And another thing,' said she, not budging, 'you'll be flying, I take it?'

'Yes. It only takes four hours or so.'

Mrs Pringle gave a short bark of a laugh.

'If you're lucky! This aunt I told you of, spent eight hours getting to Malta. First, the aeroplane needed mending, and when they started off two hours late, they found something else wrong, no petrol or one wing off – something of that – so they landed again for another two hours.'

'There's often some delay – ,' I began, but was brushed aside.

'Mind you,' said Mrs Pringle fairly, 'they give 'em something to eat while they waited. Spam and sardine sandwich – '

'What? Mixed?' I exclaimed in horror.

'That I couldn't say,' responded Mrs Pringle heavily, after thought, 'but they didn't have to pay a penny for it.'

She now made a belated foray to the dresser drawer to find a duster. Her face brightened.

'It'll keep this place tidy for a bit longer, won't it, having you away?'

Happiness comes in many guises, I thought.

Mrs Partridge, the vicar's wife, was more enthusiastic, and told me not to miss Knossos on any account – she would look out a book they had about it – and would I please take plenty of pictures so that I could give a talk or, better still, a *series* of talks to the Women's Institute when I returned.

Mr Mawne said that there was a particularly rare hawk indigenous to Crete, though he doubted if I should see one, as the Cretans probably shot every bird in sight like the blasted

Italians. Strange, he mused, that such warm-hearted people, positively *sloppy* about their children and so on, should be so callous in their treatment of animals. Anyway, he hoped I should enjoy myself, and if I were lucky enough to catch sight of the hawk then of course a few close-up photographs would be invaluable.

Mr Willet said it would do me the world of good to have some sea air and sunshine, although Barrisford would have been a sight nearer and less expensive. His cousin had been in Crete during the last war, but hadn't cared for it much as the Germans overran it while he was there and his foot was shot off in the upset.

'Still,' he added cheerfully, 'it should be nicer now the

fighting's over. I don't doubt you'll have a very good time out there.'

'Crete,' mused Mr Lamb at the Post Office. 'Now would that be the one up in the right-hand corner, shaped like a whelk?'

'Cyprus,' I said.

'Ah, then it's the one with the famous harbour, Valetta!'

'Malta,' I said.

'That so? Well, I must be getting nearer. It's not that triangular one off the toe of Italy, is it?'

'Sicily,' I said.

'Don't tell me,' begged Mr Lamb, 'I'll get it in the end. It's not one of that lot like a hatful of crabs hanging off the bottom of Greece?'

'You're getting nearer.'

'It's the long thin one,' he shouted triumphantly. 'Am I right? With some old city a chap called Sir Arthur Evans dug up with his bare hands? Our scout master told us all about it one wet evening when the cross-country run was washed out.'

'I don't know about the bare hands,' I told him, 'but the rest is right enough.'

Mrs Coggs, who had been waiting patiently to collect her family allowance, while this exchange was going on, hoped I'd have a lovely time and come back sunburnt.

Joseph, who was with her, looked alarmed.

'You *are* coming back?' he asked.

'Joseph,' I assured him, 'I'll be back.'

The next few days passed in a flurry of preparations. Amy fetched me one afternoon for a last-minute shopping spree in Caxley, as I was still unable to drive my car.

She had a wan, subdued look about her, so unlike her usual energetic manner that my heart was wrung for her. She mentioned James only once, and then simply to say that they had seen each other once or twice, and now proposed to think things over and have a discussion after the holiday.

'At least, I'm supposed to think things over,' said Amy bitterly. 'As far as I can see, his mind is made up. How this chit of a girl could have managed to get such a hold on someone as intelligent as James, I simply can't imagine!'

We were flying from Heathrow at a little after eleven in the morning, so that we did not have to make one of those dreadful journeys by car in the small hours which so often add to the traveller's discomfort.

It was one of those cold grey summer days when Amy came to collect me. A chilly wind whipped round corners, scattering a few dead leaves and wreaking havoc with our newly-arranged hair.

'I've got one of those net things with little bows all over it,' confessed Amy when we had finally stowed our baggage in the boot, and checked, yet again, passports and other documents. 'But I look like a culture-vulture from the mid-west in it, and am too vain to wear it, although it does keep one's hair tidy.'

I said I had a silk scarf if the wind became too boisterous, but I looked more like little Mother Russia in my headgear.

'Besides,' I said, 'it grieves me to pay a pound to have my hair fluffed out and then to see it flattened in five minutes.'

Rain began to fall as we approached the airport.

'Won't it be marvellous to leave all this murk behind?' crowed Amy. 'Just think of the blue skies waiting for us, and all that lovely sunshine.'

Our spirits rose, and remained high throughout the leaving of the car, the taxi ride through the tunnel, and the slow shuffle through to the departure lounge.

We found a seat, disposed our hand luggage around us, and settled down to watch our fellow travellers, and to look at the magazines we had bought to pass the time.

It was while we were thus engaged, that it suddenly dawned upon me that Amy was looking uncommonly nervous. It was the first inkling I had that she might suffer from the fear of flying.

'Do you mind flying?' I ventured.

'I loathe it,' replied Amy with some of her old energy. 'In the first place, it's dead against nature to have that great lump of metal suspended in mid-air, and no amount of sweet reasoning is going to budge that basic fact from my suspicious mind.'

'But think of the thousands and thousands of people who fly all over the place daily.'

'Lucky to be alive,' said Amy firmly. 'And think of all the hundreds who died in air crashes. I always do.'

'You shouldn't dwell on such things.'

'If you hate flying you can't help dwelling on such things! Then think of all the thousands of screws and bolts and rivets and so on, supposed to keep the bits together. How can you be sure every one of them is reliable? And what about all-over metal fatigue? Not to mention having so little time, or enough mechanics, to service the thing properly between flights.'

Amy, warming to her theme, was much more her usual forthright self, and I was pleased to see that, for a time anyway, James was forgotten.

'And then there's fire. I don't feel at all happy about all that petrol being pumped into the thing before you start off.'

'Better than forgetting it,' I pointed out. Amy ignored me.

'How does one know that there is not some ass with a cigarette drifting about nearby, and we won't all be burnt to a cinder on the tarmac?'

'There are fire tenders.'

'I daresay. With the crews in the canteen swilling coffee, and you frizzled before they can stick their axes in their belts.'

At this point, a confused noise came from the loud speakers. Someone with his head in a blanket was evidently honking down a drain-pipe. The message was quite incomprehensible to my ears, but an alert young man nearby spoke to us.

'Gate Nine, evidently.'

We collected our baggage and joined the queue.

'Well, here we go,' said Amy resignedly. 'I wonder if the pilot is a dipsomaniac?'

We settled into our seats, Amy insisting that I took the one by the window. Through it I had a view of the rear side of the wing, and beyond that the grey expanse of the airport, with only the brightly coloured tankers and aeroplanes to enliven the scene.

'Thank heaven it's daylight,' said Amy, 'and we shan't be able to see the flames shooting out of the exhausts! I face death every time I get into a blasted plane.'

'It's a quick one, I believe.'

'I wonder. I always imagine twirling round and round like a sycamore key, with one wing off.'

'Caught in the enemy's search-lights, I suppose? Amy, you've been watching too many old war films on television. Have a barley sugar, and think of Crete.'

The engines began to roar, and the aeroplane began its interminable trundling round the airport, bumping and bumbling along like some clumsy half-blind creature looking for its home.

Amy had closed her eyes, and both hands were clenched in her lap, resting on the glossy cover of a magazine which had blazoned across its corner: 'Australia: Only A Day's Flight Away'.

Suddenly, the pace of the engines altered, the roaring was terrifying, and we started to set off along what one sincerely hoped was the correct runway, and the path to Crete.

Buildings rushed past in the distance, the grass dropped away, the wing of the aeroplane dipped steeply, and far below us, tipped at an absurd angle, the streets and parks, the reservoirs and rivers of Middlesex hung like a stage backcloth.

Excitement welled in me. Amy opened her eyes and smiled.

'Well, we're off at last,' she said, with infinite relief in her voice. 'Now we can enjoy ourselves.'

The adventure had begun.

Part Two

Farther Afield

8 In Crete

OUR first glimpse of Crete was in the golden light of early evening for we had been delayed at Athens airport. It would have given Mrs Pringle some satisfaction.

If we had known how long we should have to wait for the aeroplane to Heraklion we could have taken a taxi into Athens and enjoyed a sight seeing tour. As it was, we were told at half-hourly intervals that the mechanical fault was almost repaired and we should be going aboard within minutes. Consequently, we were obliged to wait, while Amy and her fellow-sufferers grew more and more nervous, and even such phlegmatic travellers as myself grew heartily sick of cups of tepid coffee, and the appalling noise and dust made by a gang of workmen who were laying a marble floor. It was infuriating to be so near the cradle of western civilisation and yet unable to visit it, tethered as we were by the bonds of modern technology, and a pretty imperfect technology at that.

But our view of Crete from the air dispelled our irritation. There it lay, long, green and beautiful in a sea so deeply blue, that the epithet 'wine-dark' which one had accepted somewhat sceptically, was suddenly proved to be true.

Below us, like toys, small boats were crossing to and from the mainland, their white wakes echoed by the white vapour trails of an aeroplane in the blue above.

We circled lower and lower, and now we could see a white frill of waves round the bays, and white houses clustered on the green flanks of the hills. Away to the west the mountains were amethyst-coloured in the thickening light, with Mount Ida plainly to be seen.

By the time we had gone through customs, and boarded a coach, it was almost dark, and we set off eastwards along the coast road to our destination.

It was a hair-raising ride. The surface of the road – probably one of the best in the island – was remarkably rough. The coach which had met us rattled and swayed. Seats squeaked, metal jangled, windows clattered, and the driver kept up a loud conversation with our guide, only breaking off to curse any other vehicle driver foolish enough to cross his path.

We soon realised how mountainous Crete is. The main ridge of mountains runs along the central spine of the island, but the coast road too boasted some alarming ascents and descents. Part of our journey was along a newly built road, but there was still much to be done, and we followed the path used by generations of travellers from Heraklion to Aghios Nikolaos for most of the way.

The last part of the journey took place in darkness. The headlights lit up the white villages through which we either hurtled down or laboured up. Occasionally, we saw a tethered goat cropping busily beneath the brilliant stars, or a pony clopping along at the side of the road, its rider muffled in a rough cloak.

Every now and again the coach shuddered to a halt, and a few passengers descended, laden with luggage, to find their hotel.

'I wouldn't mind betting,' said Amy, with a yawn, 'that we are the last to be put down.'

She would have lost her bet, but only just, for we were the penultimate group to be dropped. Two middle-aged couples, and a family of five struggled from the coach with us and we made our way through a courtyard to the doorway.

We were all stiff and tired for we had been travelling since morning. A delicious aroma was floating about the entrance hall. It was as welcome as the smiles of the men behind the desk.

'Grub!' sighed one of our fellow-travellers longingly.

He echoed the feelings of us all.

School teachers do not usually stay in expensive hotels, so that I was all the more impressed with the beauty and efficiency of the one we now inhabited.

The gardens were extensive and followed the curve of the bay. Evergreen trees and flowering shrubs scented the air, lilies and cannas and orange blossom adding their perfume. And everywhere water trickled, irrigating the thirsty ground, and adding its own rustling music to that of the sea which splashed only a few yards from our door.

Amy and I shared a little whitewashed stone house, comprising one large room with two beds and some simple wooden furniture, a bathroom and a spacious verandah where we had breakfast each morning. The rest of the meals were taken in the main part of the hotel to which we walked along brick paths, sniffing so rapturously at all the plants that Amy said I looked like Ferdinand the bull.

'Heavens! That dates us,' I said. 'I haven't thought of Ferdinand for about thirty years!'

'Must be more than that,' said Amy. 'It was before the war. Isn't it strange how one's life is divided into before and after wars? I used to get so mad with my parents telling me about all the wonderful things they could buy for two and eleven-three before 1914 that I swore I would never do the same thing, but I do. I heard myself telling Vanessa, only the other day, what a hard-wearing winter coat I had bought for thirty shillings *before the war*. She didn't seem to believe me, I must say.'

'It's at times like Christmas that I hark back,' I confessed. 'I used to reckon to buy eight presents for college friends for a pound. Dash it all, you could get a silk scarf or a real leather purse for half a crown in those days.'

'And a swansdown powder puff sewn into a beautiful square

of crêpe-de-chine,' sighed Amy. 'Ah, well! No good living in the past. I must say the present suits me very well. Do you think I'm burning?'

We were lying by the swimming pool after breakfast. Already the sun was hot. By eleven it would be too hot to sunbathe, and we should find a shady place under the trees or on our own verandah, listening to the lazy splashing of the waves on the rocks.

On the terrace above us four gardeners were tending two minute patches of coarse grass. A sprinkler played upon these tiny lawns for most of the day. Sometimes an old-fashioned lawn-mower would be run over them, with infinite care. The love which was lavished upon these two shaggy patches should have produced something as splendidly elegant as the lawns at the Backs in Cambridge, one felt, but to Cretan eyes, no doubt, the result was as satisfying.

For the first two or three days we were content to loll in the sun, to bathe in the hotel pool, and to potter about the enchanting town of Aghios Nikolaos. We were both tired. My arm was still in a sling for most of the time, and pained me occasionally if I moved it at an awkward angle. Amy's troubles were far harder to bear, and I marvelled at her courage in thrusting them out of sight. We were both anxious that the other should benefit from the holiday, and as we both liked the same things we were in perfect accord.

'We'll hire a car,' Amy said, 'for the rest of the holiday. There are so many lovely things to see. First trip to Knossos, and I think we'll make an early start on that day. It was hot enough there when I went in April. Heaven knows what it will be like in August!'

Meanwhile, we slept and ate and bathed and read, glorying

in the sunshine, the shimmering heat, the blue, blue sea and the sheer joy of being somewhere different.

Now and again I felt a pang of remorse as I thought of Tibby in her hygienic surroundings at the super-kennels to which I had taken her. No doubt she loathed the comfortable bed provided, the dried cat-food, the fresh water, and the concrete run thoughtfully washed out daily with weak disinfectant by her kind warders.

Where, she would be wondering, is the garden, and my lilac tree scratching post? Where is the grass I like to eat, and my comfortably dirty blanket, and the dishes of warm food put down by a doting owner?

It would not do Tibby any harm, I told myself, to have a little discipline for two weeks. She would appreciate her home comforts all the more keenly when we were reunited.

Our fellow guests seemed a respectable collection of folk. In the main, they were middle-aged, and enjoying themselves in much the same way as Amy and I were. There were one or two families with older children, but no babies to be seen. I assumed that there were a number of reasons for this lack of youth.

The hotel was expensive, and to take two or three children there for a fortnight or so would be beyond most families' purses. The natural bathing facilities were not ideal for youngsters. The coast was rocky, the beaches small and often shelving abruptly. The flight from England was fairly lengthy, and it was easy to see why there were very few small children about.

It suited me. I like children well enough, otherwise I should not be teaching, but enough is enough, and part of the pleasure of this particular holiday was the company of adults only.

We looked forward to a short time in the bar after dinner, talking to other guests and sometimes watching the Greek waiters who had been persuaded to dance. We loved the gravity of these local dances as, arms resting on each others' shoulders, the young men swooped in unison, legs swinging backwards and forwards, their dark faces solemn with concentration, until, at last, they would finish with a neat acrobatic leap to face the other way, and their smiles would acknowledge our applause.

One of the middle-aged couples who had made the journey with us, often came to sit with us in the bar. Their stone house was near our own, and we often found ourselves walking to dinner together through the scented darkness.

She was small and neat, with prematurely white silky hair, worn in soft curls. Blue-eyed and fair-skinned she must have been enchanting as a girl, and even now, in middle-age, her elegance was outstanding. She dressed in white or blue, accentuating the colour of her hair and eyes, and wore a brooch and bracelet of sapphires and pearls which even I coveted.

Her husband looked much younger, with a shock of crisp dark hair, a slim bronzed figure, and a ready flow of conversation. We found them very good company.

'The Clarks,' Amy said to me one evening, as we dressed for dinner, 'remind me of the advertisement for pep pills. You know: "Where do they get their energy?" They seem so wonderfully in tune too. I must say, it turns the knife in the wound at times,' she added, with a tight smile.

'Well, they're not likely to parade any secret clashes before other people staying here,' I pointed out reasonably.

'True enough,' agreed Amy. 'Half the fun of hotel life is speculating about one's neighbours. What do you think of the two who bill and coo at the table on our left?'

'Embarrassing,' I said emphatically. 'Must have been married for years, and still stroking hands while they wait for their soup. Talk about washing one's clean linen in public!'

'They may have been married for years,' said Amy, in what I have come to recognise as her worldly-woman voice, 'but was it to each other?'

'Miaow!' I intoned.

Amy laughed.

'You trail the innocence of Fairacre wherever you go,' she teased. 'And not a bad thing either.'

It was the morning after this conversation that I found my-self dozing alone, frying nicely, under some trees near the pool. Amy was writing cards on the verandah, and was to join me later.

I heard footsteps approach, and opened my eyes to see Mrs Clark smiling at me.

'Can I share the shade?'

'Of course.' I shifted along obligingly, and Mrs Clark spread a rug and cushion, and arranged herself elegantly upon them.

'John's in the pool, but it does mess up one's hair so, that I thought I'd miss my dip today. How is your arm?'

I assured her that I was mending fast.

'It's all this lovely fresh air and sunshine,' she said. 'It's a heavenly climate. My husband would like to live here.'

'I can understand it.'

'So can I. He has more reason than most to like the Greek way of life. His grandmother was a Greek. She lived a few miles south of Athens, and John spent a number of holidays with her as a schoolboy.'

'Lucky fellow!'

'I suppose so.' She sounded sad, and I wondered what lay behind this disclosure.

'We visited her, as often as we could manage it, right up to her death about five or six years ago. A wonderful old lady. She had been a widow for years. In fact, I never met John's grandfather. He died when John was still at Marlborough.'

She sat up and anointed one slim leg with sun tan lotion. Her expression was serious, as she worked away. I began to suspect, with some misgiving, that once again I was destined to hear someone's troubles.

'You see,' she went on, 'John retires from the Army next year, and he is set on coming here to live. He's even started house-hunting.'

'And what do you feel about it?'

She turned a defiant blue gaze upon me.

'I'm dead against it. I'm moving heaven and earth to try to get him to change his mind, and I intend to succeed. It's a dream he has lived with for years – first it was to live in Athens. Then in one or other of the Greek islands, and now it's definitely whittled down to Crete. I've never seen him so ruthless.'

I thought of Amy who had used almost exactly the same words about James.

'Perhaps something will occur to make him change his mind,' I suggested.

'Never! He's thought of this kind of life wherever he's been, and I feel that he's been through so much that it is right in a way for him to have what he wants, now that he will have the leisure to enjoy it. But the thing is, I can't bear the thought of it. We should have to leave everything behind that we love, I tell him.'

She began to attack the other leg with ferocity.

'We live in Surrey. Over the years we saved enough to buy this rather nice house, with a big garden, and we've been lucky enough to live in it for the past seven years. Before that, of course, we were posted here, there, and everywhere, but one expects that. I thought that John had given up the idea of settling out here. He's seemed so happy helping me in the garden, and making improvements to the house. Now I realise that he was looking upon the place as something valuable to sell to finance a home here. And the garden – ,'

She broke off, and bent low, ostensibly to examine her leg.

'Tell me about it,' I said.

'I've made a heavenly rockery. It slopes steeply, and you can get some very good terraces cut into the side of the hill. My gentians are doing so well, and lots of little Alpines. And three years ago I planted an autumn flowering prunus which had lots of blossom last October – so pretty. I simply *won't* leave it!'

'You could make a garden here I expect. My friend Amy tells me that when she was here last, in April, there were carnations and geraniums, and lilies of all sorts. Think of that!'

'And then there are the grandchildren,' she went on, as though she had not heard me. 'We have two girls, both married, who live quite near us, and we see the grandchildren several times a week. There are three, and a new baby due soon after we return. I'm going to keep house for Irene when she goes into hospital, and look after her husband and Bruce, the first boy.'

'You'll enjoy that, I expect,' I said, hoping to wean her from her unhappiness. I did not succeed.

'But just think of all those little things growing up miles away from us! Think of the fun we're going to miss, seeing them at all the different stages! I keep reminding John of this. And then there's Podge.'

'Podge?'

'Our spaniel. He's nearly twelve and far too old to settle overseas, in a hot climate. Irene has offered to have him, but he would grieve without us, and I should grieve too, I don't deny. No, it can't be done.'

She looked at me, and smiled.

'I really shouldn't be worrying you with my problems, but you have such a sympathetic face, you know.'

This is not the first time I have been told this. I cannot help feeling that my face works independently of my inner thoughts. It certainly seems to make me the repository of all kinds of unsolicited confidences, as I know to my cost.

'I'm quite sure,' she continued, screwing on the stopper of the lotion bottle, 'that my daughters wouldn't be putting up with this situation. For one thing, of course, they could be financially independent, a thing I've never been.'

'Even if you were,' I said cautiously, 'you wouldn't part from your husband surely?'

'No, I suppose not.' She sounded doubtful. 'There's been no choice, of course. I wasn't brought up to do a job of any kind, and I married fairly young. Now I suppose I am virtually unemployable. I must stay with John, or starve.'

She laughed, rather tremulously, and hastened to skate away from this thin ice. She spoke firmly.

'No, of course, I wouldn't leave him. We really are devoted

to each other, and he is a wonderful husband. It's just this terrible problem . . .'

Her voice trailed away. Sighing, she lay down again, and stretched herself, enjoying the warm air, heavy with the scent of orange blossom.

Far away a gull cried, and water slapped rhythmically against a wooden boat moored by the little stone jetty. It seemed sad to me that such an earthly paradise should be spoilt for this poor woman by the cloud of worries which surrounded her.

One's first thought was how selfish her husband was to insist on disrupting her happy domesticity.

On the other hand he had served his country well presumably, had been uprooted time and time again in the course of his duties, and surely he was entitled to spend his retirement in the place he had always loved.

A pity they were married, I thought idly. Separately, they could have been so happy – she in Surrey, he in Crete. Or would they have been? Obviously, they loved each other. She would not be suffering so if she were not concerned for his happiness.

Ah well! There was a lot to be said for being single. One might miss a great deal, but at least one's life was singularly uncomplicated.

Side by side, spinster and spouse, we both slipped into slumber, as the sun climbed the Cretan sky.

9 At Knossos

THE night before our trip to Knossos we had a thunder-storm, frightening in its intensity.

Normally, I enjoy a thunderstorm at night when the black sky is cracked with silver shafts, and sheet lightning illumines the downs with an eerie flickering. Nature at her most dramatic can be very exhilarating, but a Mediterranean storm was much more alarming, I discovered, than the Fairacre variety.

The sea had become turbulent by the time we undressed for bed. The usual gentle lapping sound was transmuted to noisy crashes. Our little stone house, so solidly built, seemed to shudder in the onslaught from the sea.

But soon the noise of the waves was lost in the din of the storm. Thunder rumbled and cracked like a whip overhead. The lightning seemed continuous, turning the bay into a grotesquely coloured stage-set, against which the moored boats jostled and dipped like drunken men trying to stay up-right.

The rain came down like rods. Everything glistened, roofs, walls, trees and flowers. And everywhere there was the sound of running water. It poured from gutters, rushed down slopes, turning the brick paths to rivers, and washing the carefully garnered soil down to the sea below.

'You can't wonder,' shouted Amy, above the din, from her

bed, 'that the Greeks made sacrifices to propitiate the gods when they thought they were responsible for all this racket. I wouldn't mind pouring out a libation myself, to stop the noise.'

'No oil or wine available,' I shouted back, 'unless you care for a saucerful of my suntan oil.'

'We may as well put on the light and read,' said Amy, sitting up. 'Sleep's impossible.'

Propped against our pillows we studied our books. At least, Amy did.

She was zealously preparing for tomorrow's trip by reading a guide to Knossos. Amy's powers of concentration far outstrip my own, and despite the ferocity of the storm outside, she was soon deeply engrossed.

Less dedicated, I turned the pages of one of the magazines we had brought with us, and wondered how Fairacre would react if, salary allowing, I appeared in some of the autumn outfits displayed. What about this rust-coloured woollen two-piece trimmed with red fox? Just the thing for writing on the blackboard. Or this elegant pearl-grey frock banded with chinchilla? The plasticine would settle in that beautifully.

'Do you imagine anyone ever buys these things?' I asked, yawning. 'Or do they all go to Marks and Spencer, and their local outfitter's as we do?'

Amy looked vaguely in my direction. One could see her mind gradually returning from 2000 B.C. to the present time.

'Of course someone wears them,' she replied. 'I've even had some myself when James has been feeling extra generous.'

She drew in her breath sharply. She was once again firmly in the present with all its hurts and its hopes. I cursed myself for disturbing her reading and its temporary comfort.

'Listen,' I said, 'the storm is going away.'

It was true. The rain had become a mere pattering. The thunder was a distant rumbling, the spouting of gutters diminished to a trickle.

Amy smiled and closed her book.

'That *silly* man,' she said lovingly. 'I wonder what he's doing?'

She slid down under the bedclothes and was asleep in three minutes, leaving me to marvel at the inconsistency of women.

The morning was brilliant. Everything glittered in its freshness after the storm, and the sea air was more than usually exhilarating.

We piled our belongings into the hired mini which was to carry us to Knossos, and a score of other places, during the rest of our stay. It was the cheapest vehicle we could hire, and privately I thought the sum asked was outrageous, but Amy did not turn a hair on being told the terms, and once again I was deeply conscious of her generosity to me.

'Let's lunch in Heraklion,' said Amy, 'and have a look at the museum first. Most of the things are of the Minoan period. I must have another look at the ivory acrobat, and spend more time looking at the jewellery which is simply lovely. Last time, we spent far too long gazing at frescoes, and to my mind, it's the small things which are so fascinating.'

Her enthusiasm was catching, and we drove westward towards Crete's capital in high spirits. The mini coped well with the rough surfaces and the steep gradients, and I felt considerably safer with Amy at the wheel than I had with our first coach driver.

Heraklion teemed with traffic, but Amy found a car park,

with her usual competence, not far from the museum, so that all was well.

It was a wonderful building, with the exhibits well arranged, and everything bathed in that pellucid light which blesses the Greek islands. Amy and I started our tour together, but gradually drifted apart, enjoying the exquisite workmanship of almost four thousand years ago, at our own pace. I left her studying the jewellery while I went upstairs.

I could see why she and James had spent so long admiring the frescoes on their earlier visit. There was such pride and gaiety in the processions of men and women on the walls. Sport was depicted everywhere, vaulting, leaping, running, wrestling; and the famous bulls of Crete were shown in all their powerful splendour by the Minoan artists.

We spent two hours there, dazed and awed, by so much magnificence.

'What we need,' said Amy, when we met again, 'is two or three months in this place.'

'But first of all, lunch,' I said.

We crossed the road to some shops and cafés which seemed to have tables set out on the pavement under shady awnings. We were met by three or four garrulous proprietors, each rubbing and clapping his hands, pointing out the superior quality of his own establishment, and the extreme pleasure which he would have in receiving our custom. The noise was deafening, and the constant stream of traffic made it worse.

We were practically tugged into one café and settled meekly at the paper-covered table. A large dark hand brushed the remains of someone else's lunch to the ground, and a menu was thrust before us.

'All sorts of salads,' observed Amy, studying it closely, 'or

95

something called "Pork's Livers Roasted" and another one named "Chick's Rice Fried". Unless you fancy "Heart's Beefs Noodled".'

I said I would settle for shrimp salad. We had soon discovered that the shrimps of Crete are as succulent as prawns, and much the same size. We were fast becoming shrimp addicts.

'Me too,' said Amy, giving our order to the beaming proprietor.

An American couple were deposited suddenly in the two empty chairs opposite us. They looked apologetic, as their captor rushed away to rescue the menu.

'I hope you two ladies don't object to us being thrust upon you,' said the man earnestly. 'We didn't intend to have lunch here, but were kinda captured.'

We said we had been too.

'One comfort,' said Amy, 'the food looks very good.'

'I'm sure glad to hear that,' said the man. 'I can eat most anything, but Mrs Judd here has a highly sensitive stomach, and is a sufferer from gas. Ain't that so, Mother?' he said, bending solicitously towards his wife, who was studying our fellow diners' plates with the deepest suspicion.

Mother, who must have weighed fourteen stone and had a mouth like Mrs Pringle's, with the corners turned down, was understood to say she couldn't relish anything in this joint, and how about pushing on?

Her husband consulted a large square watch on a hairy wrist, and surmised time was on the short side if they wanted to take in Knossos, and get back again for shopping, before meeting the Hyams for a drink at 6 o'clock. He guessed this place was as good as the next, and at least they were at the table, no lining up like that goddam place they went to yesterday, so why not make the best of it?

Mother pouted.

Of course, said her husband swiftly, if Mother was real set on going elsewhere, why, that was fine by him! Just whatever Mother wanted.

At that moment the menu arrived.

'Beefs very good. Porks very Good. Chicks very good. Salads very good,' chanted the waiter, his eyes darting this way and that in quest of yet more clients.

'What you two girls having?' asked Mother grumpily.

'Shrimp salad,' we chorused.

'That'll do me, Abe,' she said, 'the tomaytoes are certainly fine in this country. You got tomaytoes?' she added anxiously.

'Plenty tomaytoes,' nodded the waiter. 'Tomaytoes very good. You like?'

'I'll have the same,' said Abe.

The waiter vanished. Abe patted Mother's hand, and beamed upon her.

'You certainly know what you like,' he said proudly. If she had suddenly explained Einstein's theory he could not have been more respectful.

Our shrimp salads arrived, and Abe and Mother studied them as we ate. They were delicious, and soon a mound of heads and tails grew at the side of our enormous white plates.

A thin white cat weaved her way from the shop through the legs of the chairs, and sat close to us.

With thoughts of my incarcerated Tibby, I handed down a few shrimp heads. There was a rapid crunching, and the pavement was clear again. I repeated the process. So did the cat.

'Like a miniature Hoover,' commented Amy.

'Starving, poor thing,' said Mother. 'Or got some wasting disease maybe.'

'I haven't seen any animals looking hungry in Crete,' I said, coming to the defence of our hosts. 'Cats in hot climates often look thin to our eyes.'

'I was raised where cats were kept in their place,' said Mother. 'If us kids had fed our animals at the table, we'd have caught the rough side of our Pa's tongue.'

I forbore to comment.

'You ladies aiming at going to Knossos?' asked Abe, changing the subject with aplomb.

We said we were.

'You done the museum?'

We said we had.

'Some beautiful things there,' said Mother, 'but I didn't care for the ladies in the wall-paintings. Shocking to think they went topless like any disgusting modern girl. I sure was thankful our Pastor wasn't present. What did you think, Abe?'

Abe looked uncomfortable.

'Well, I thought they were proper handsome. Fine upstanding girls they looked to me.'

Mother gave him a stern look.

'After all,' said Abe pleadingly, 'it was a long time back. Maybe they didn't know any better.'

At that moment, their plates arrived, and we asked for our bill and paid it.

'See you at Knossos!' shouted Abe, as we said our farewells and walked away from the table.

'Do you take that as a threat or a promise?' asked Amy, when we were safely out of earshot.

As luck would have it, we did not come across our friends at Knossos, but Amy commented on them as we parked the car at the gates at the site of the ruined palace.

'I wonder how many English wives would be pandered to as Mother is,' she mused.

'Would they want it?'

'On the whole, no. On the other hand, it must be wonderfully encouraging to be deferred to so often. It might make one terribly selfish, of course. After all, it hasn't done Mother a lot of good – sulking like a spoilt child when things go wrong.'

'Perhaps they haven't any children,' I surmised. 'Couples without children often get over-possessive with each other.'

'Not all of them,' said Amy dryly. And I remembered – too late as usual – that she and James were childless. Whoever it was called the tongue an unruly member was certainly right. Trying to control my own proves wellnigh impossible, and results in more self-reproach than I care to admit.

'Or perhaps,' I continued hastily, 'it's a case of arrested development, and Abe panders to her simply because she's so immature.'

'Immature? Mother?' snorted Amy, locking the car door with a decisive click. 'Mother's development has reached its highest peak, for what it's worth. She's got that man exactly where she wants him – under her thumb. Whether it makes her happy or not is another thing, but you see it over and over again in marriages. One must be boss; never an equal partnership.'

We made our way in the brilliant sunshine to the entrance to Knossos.

'You make marriage sound a hazardous proceeding,' I remarked. 'I don't think I could have succeeded in it.'

Amy shook her head at me.

'You don't know what you've missed, my girl. It has a bright side, believe me. I'll tell you all about it one day. I bet even Abe and Mother have a few happy times.'

'Well, let's hope they enjoyed their shrimp salads. I don't like to think of Mother suffering with gas while she's sightseeing.'

We entered the grounds, and made our way through a shady avenue which led uphill to the site of the great palace, where men and women, some two thousand years B.C., had faced, no doubt, the same marital problems at large today.

I had no idea, when reading about Knossos, how vast an area the whole concourse covered. As before, Amy and I started our tour together, but soon decided to meet, two hours hence, at the gate, for there was so much to see that one was better on one's own.

As always, it was the light that impressed me most. It was easy to see how such a happy civilisation evolved. The clarity of light, the warmth of the sun and the embracing sea, combined to give an exhilaration of spirit. Fertile soil, many rivers and trees were an added blessing. Small wonder that the ancient Minoans had a spontaneous gaiety and energy which created such a wealth of superb architecture, paintings and sculpture.

They were practical people too, I was glad to see, with sensible plumbing, spacious bathrooms and plenty of storage space for their provisions. Many a twentieth century builder in England, I thought, could have learnt a thing or two from the workmen of Minoan Crete.

The great staircases, supported by the massive red columns, smaller at the base than the top, led from one floor to another, and on each were things to stand and marvel at. A little crowd stood looking at King Minos' throne, reckoned to be the oldest in the world. But the object which gave me most pleasure was the fresco in the Queen's room showing dolphins at sport above the entrance. There they play, some four thousand years old, still bearing that particularly endearing expression of benignity which so enchants us when we see the fish today cavorting, for our delight, in water parks and zoos.

Their gaiety was echoed in the frescoes showing processions or feats of physical skill. Many we had seen in the museum, but replicas were here, and one could not help but be impressed with the physical beauty and elegance of the men and women. The topless gowns, so frowned upon by Mother, had beautiful bell-shaped skirts, and the stiff bodices, cut away to expose the breasts, supported them and were intricately adorned with gold and precious jewels. Their hair was long and wavy, their eyes made up as lavishly as Vanessa's. They were really the most decorative creatures, and not above helping in the acrobatic pursuits, as the pictures of them assisting their menfolk in the bull-vaulting escapades showed clearly.

Perhaps, I mused, this is what northerners lack. Our climate is against flimsy clothing, sea-bathing and outdoor sports. If we took more physical exercise, should we be more blithe and energetic? Would our lives become as creative and as happy as the Minoans' most certainly were? Should we be less introspective, less prone to self-pity, less critical of others?

The secret, I decided, was simply in the sun. Given that, given warmth and light, one was more than half-way to happiness.

I rose from my staircase seat looking out to sea, and made my way reluctantly to the outside world.

'But I shall come again,' I said aloud, stroking the ancient dust from a pillar as I passed. There was so much more to learn from the Minoans about the proper way to live.

10 Amy Works Things Out

'IT is a truth universally acknowledged,' Jane Austen tells us, 'that a single man in possession of a good fortune must be in want of a wife.'

A lesser truth, universally acknowledged, is that the first week of a fortnight's holiday is twice as long as the second week. Why this should be so remains a mystery, but no doubt the theory of relativity might throw some light on the matter if one could only understand it.

'Of course,' say some people, trying to be rational, 'one *does* so much the first week. Trips here and there, friends to visit, new people to meet – it's bound to seem longer.'

But this theory did not apply to Amy and me. Apart from the trip to Knossos, and some blissful walks in the mountains after the main heat of the day had passed, we had done nothing but sleep, bathe, eat and converse in a languid fashion. True, we had roused ourselves to write a few postcards, now and again, but on the whole the first week had seemed like two days, and here we were, embarking on our second week, with dozens of places as yet unvisited.

Aghios Nikolaos itself we quartered fairly thoroughly, for we had taken to shopping for our midday picnic, collecting a hot fragrant loaf from the bakery in a cobbled side street, choosing cheese and chocolate, but learning quickly to wait until we reached the villages to buy the famous tomatoes, for here, in the town's dusty streets, their freshness soon withered. We soon knew the most welcoming cafés, the newsagent who sold English newspapers, the shoe-maker who would make you a pair of leather sandals in next to no time, and the jewellers who displayed the beautiful gold filigree work which was beyond even Amy's purse.

But it was life in the country, in the small villages among the olive groves and the carob trees, which fascinated us.

Despite the splendid electric lights which hung in some of the narrow streets, most of the houses seemed to have none indoors. The interiors were dark, and the families seemed to sit on their doorsteps as long as the light lasted.

We met them, during the day, and particularly in the early evening, on their way home. The little groups usually consisted of a man and wife, and perhaps one or two children. They would be accompanied by a mule or a donkey, sometimes both, and two or three goats. Occasionally, a cow swaggered indolently with them, its full bag swaying from side to side. The animals were in fine condition, and the American, Mother, was quite wrong to accuse the Cretans of callousness. All those we saw were lovingly tended, and the sheepdogs that sometimes ran with the family were as lively as those at Fairacre.

Always there would be a great bundle of greenery, culled from the banks, for the beasts' evening fodder, and always too, a large bundle of kindling wood lodged across the front of the donkey's saddle, intended, no doubt, for cooking the evening meal.

The women were dressed in black, and the men in clothes of dark material. All acknowledged us when we met, and smiled in a friendly way, but it was quite apparent that they were busy.

They were at work. They wished us well but would not dally. Here, the Biblical way of life still held – a day to day existence, charted by the hours of light and darkness, and by the swing of the seasons. There was a serenity about these people which we have lost it seems. Perhaps we have too many possessions, look too far ahead, take 'too much thought for the morrow, what we shall eat, what we shall put on'. Amy and I would not have wanted to change to this style of living, even if we could, but it was balm to our spirits to see the simplicity and dignity of another way of life, and to learn from it.

We decided to visit the monastery of Toplou at the far eastern end of the island. We had soon realised that it was impossible to attempt to see the western half of Crete, for the hilly nature of the country and the surface of many of the roads made the going slow.

'We'll come again,' promised Amy, 'and we'll stay in Heraklion next time, and push westward from there.'

Meanwhile we intended to see as much as we could with Aghios Nikolaos as our very good centre. The coast road eastward, we soon discovered, on the morning we set off for Toplou, had its own hazards, for falls of rock had crashed into the road and gangs of workmen shook their heads and did their best to stop us.

Amy was at her most persuasive, and tried to explain that we should never be so foolhardy as to run into real danger, but surely, if they themselves were brave enough to be working on the road then our little car – driven with *infinite* care – could edge past?

They grimaced at us, poured forth a torrent of Greek to each other, held up their elbows and looked fearfully above them, miming the dangers we must expect if we persisted. We sat and smiled at them, nodding to show we understood, and at last, with a shrugging of shoulders, they beckoned us on. Their expressions showed clearly their feelings. On our own heads be it – and that might well be, literally, a ton or two of overhanging rock, made unsafe by the violent storm of a few nights before.

We survived. The sky was overcast that day, but the sea air lifted our hair, and we sat on short turf which smelt aromatically of thyme, to have our picnic.

'I wonder,' said Amy lazily, as we rested after lunch, 'what the outcome will be between the Clarks. She came round this morning, when you were up at the hotel, to borrow the Knossos guide book. Do you know, that wretched man thinks he's found a house! She's beside herself.'

'Where is the house?'

'Malia.'

I remembered it as one of the ancient sites on the road to Heraklion. I also remembered it as a dusty, somewhat sleazy, long street full of booths selling straw hats, and bags, and some pretty fearful souvenirs. I couldn't see Mrs Clark settling there after the green and pleasant purlieus of Surrey.

'What's her reaction?' I asked.

'Unusually forceful, which I think's a good thing. He's gone a little too far a little too quickly, and while she was really doing her best to meet him halfway a week ago, now she's beginning to get much tougher.'

'What a problem! I only hope they don't fall out permanently. They seem so fond of each other, that I can't see them getting too vicious over this affair.'

'I'm sure they'll find some solution. Evidently, she now stipulates that nothing is bought outright until they have lived

in the place for a few months, and can see how they like it.'

'Seems sensible. So he's agreed to rent something?'

'I don't know. The difficulty is that people move step by step into awkward positions, and then won't swallow their pride and climb down.'

'Too true.'

'Look at James. I really can't believe that he wants to spend the rest of his life with this girl. She'll bore him to tears by the end of the year.'

'You know her then?' I was taken by surprise. Amy had said so little about the girl that I had jumped to the conclusion that James had met her somewhere on his travels.

'I've met her a few times in James's office. She's one of his typists. Perfectly nice child, I imagine, but should be flirting with some cheerful young man at her local tennis club or dramatic society – not ogling her boss.'

Amy stubbed out a cigarette viciously among the thymy grass.

'If this had happened twenty or thirty years ago,' she went on, 'I should have tackled it quite differently.

'I keep remembering my Aunt Winifred who coped with much the same situation when she was my age. Did I ever tell you about it?'

'No,' I said, settling comfortably for a domestic saga. 'Tell on.'

'Well, soon after I left college I had a couple of years at a rather nice school near Highbury. As my Aunt Winifred lived close by, my parents, after much heart-searching, asked her if I might stay there as a P.G.

'She was a game old girl, and had no children of her own, and said of course I must stay there, which I did, going home at weekends. Incidentally, she refused to take a penny in rent which made my upright parents most uncomfortable, but there it was.

'My uncle Peter was an accountant – perhaps book-keeper is nearer the mark – at one of the good London stores, Harrods or Jacksons, something of the sort. He caught the 8.10 train every morning and came into the house between 6.30 and 7 every evening. He was very sweet and gentle, and always brought us a cup of tea in bed in the mornings, and spent his spare time pottering about in his greenhouse.

'Imagine then, the horror when he calmly asked Aunt Winifred if she would kindly remove herself as he wished to bring home "*a very lady-like girl*" – I can hear my poor Aunt Win mimicking his tone to this day – whom he hoped to marry as soon as he and Aunt Winifred could get a divorce.

'I was not present, naturally, at this scene, but heard all about it from my aunt some time later.'

'What on earth did she do?'

'You'll be amazed. As amazed as I was, all those years ago, I expect. She told me this with a smile of such self-satisfaction on her face that I was rendered speechless at the time. It seems that she had been left a small legacy by a godfather not long before. Something in the region of two hundred pounds. When she was telling me this, I remember thinking: "Oh, what a good thing! She could make a start somewhere else!" But I realised that she was telling me that she decided to use the money "to win him back". She proposed to ignore his suggestion completely, but do you know what she did?'

'Bought him back with two hundred?'

'As near as! She blew the lot on having her hair dyed and re-styled. She bought masses of new clothes. She had a face-lift and heaven knows what else. Then she calmly waited for him to fall in love with her all over again.'

'And did he?'

'I think not. He was even more subdued after that little escapade; but she did succeed as she intended to do.'

Amy sighed.

'You can imagine my feelings on hearing this tale. I was absolutely furious. At that age I thought I should have let the man have his way, and gone off myself, rejoicing in the two hundred which would keep me going until I found a suitable job. To crawl around trying to get him back was the last thing I should have done. I was so shocked by my aunt's attitude that I said nothing. Perhaps it was as well.'

'And how do you feel now about it?'

Amy looked at me steadily.

'I'm thirty years older and wiser. I know now how Aunt Winifred felt. To put it at its lowest level first – why should she give up her bed and board, and all the settled ways of a lifetime simply because he wanted to opt out of a solemn contract they had made? Why should she – the innocent party – shatter her own life simply because he wanted to be unfaithful?

'On a slightly less material plane, she realised, I know, – and now that I'm facing the same problem I know how much it hurts – that one can't just destroy a shared life by walking away. The memories, the experiences, the influences one has had on the other, have simply made you what you are, and they can never be completely wiped out.'

Amy reached for a piece of grass and began to nibble it thoughtfully. Her voice was steady, her eyes dry. It seemed to me that this outpouring was the fruit of much suffering and tension. One could only hope it would give her relief, and I was glad to be able to play the role of passive friend.

'And then, of course, Aunt Winifred was a religious woman and took her marriage vows seriously. When she was told that God had joined them together and that no man, or woman, should put them asunder, then she believed it without a shadow of doubt. I'm sure she stuck to Uncle Peter as she did because she felt sure he would be committing a mortal sin and must be saved from this truly wicked temptation. She told herself – as God knows I've told myself often enough – that this was a kind of madness which would pass if she could only hold on.'

Amy threw away her ruined grass stalk.

'And she did, and the marriage held, and I don't think she ever chided Uncle Peter about the affair. But for all that, it could never be quite the same again. You can't be hurt as much as that and get away without the scars.'

There was a little silence, broken only by the mewing of a seagull, balancing in the air nearby.

'And will you hold on?' I ventured.

Amy nodded slowly.

'I've learnt that much from Aunt Winifred. In the end, the outcome may not be the same, but I've more sense now, than I had thirty years ago, than to fling off in high independence and precipitate things.'

She turned to me suddenly and smiled.

'And another thing, I'm so awfully fond of the silly old man. We've shared too much and for too long to be pettish with each other. I'm not throwing that away lightly. That's the real stuff of marriage which you lucky old spinsters, with your nice uncomplicated lives, can't appreciate. It's an enrichment. It's fun. It's absorbing – more so, I imagine, if you have a family – and so you just don't destroy it, but nurture it.'

She sprang to her feet, took my one good hand in hers and heaved me upright.

'Come along, Nelson,' she said, as I adjusted my sling. 'Toplou is some way off. Think of those fortunate monks who have no such problems as mine!'

We piled the remains of our picnic into the basket, and picked our way back to the car.

Amy's spirits had recovered. She chanted as we headed eastward:

> '*And miles to go before I sleep*
> '*And miles to go before I sleep.*'

11 Toplou

THE monastery of Toplou stood like a fortress silhouetted against the grey sky. We approached it by a tortuous road, snaking up the hillside.

The wind grew stronger as we ascended, and a fine drizzle of rain misted the windscreen. At the summit, we drove across bumpy grass into a deserted forecourt.

The wind buffeted us as we emerged from the car, and went towards the cliffs' edge. We stood on a headland, the dark sea hundreds of feet below us clawing with white foamy tentacles at the rocks below. Sea-birds screamed and wheeled, floating like scraps of paper in the eddies of wind. It was too rough to talk. The wind blew into our mouths, snatching words away, making us gasp with shock.

There was no one in sight. A disused mill, sails gone, and one salt-bleached door hanging awry, stood nearby. At its footings, a dozen or so scrawny chickens scratched and pecked, scurrying away with clucks of alarm, as we struggled by them.

It was more sheltered in the courtyard, but equally deserted. A verandah ran round the four sides, at first floor level, and large rusty tins were ranged at intervals. Once they had acted as window boxes, it would seem, but now, rust-streaked and battered, only a few dead stock plants protruded from them.

Everywhere the paint was flaking, and the walls were

streaked with the rain-trickles of many seasons. This famous
Christian monastery, built by the Venetians 600 years earlier
to withstand the assaults of the infidel Turks across the water,
presented a pathetic sight close to, in contrast with the magnificence of its aspect when viewed from afar.

We approached a door and knocked. There was no sign of
life. We looked about us as we waited. Someone, somewhere,
lived in this sad place. A tattered tea towel flapped from a
make-shift wire line, destined never to dry whilst the misty air
encompassed all.

We knocked again, louder this time, but with the same result.
Disconsolate, we began to explore further. A dark archway
seemed to lead to another courtyard. A broom was propped
against a wall. A bucket stood nearby. Were those potato
peelings in its murky depths?

We tried another door. This time we began to open it
gently after our preliminary knocks had brought no answer.
The handle was rough and gritty to our touch, eroded by the
salt air, clammy in our palms.

'May we come in?' we cried into the twilit room.

There was a responsive rumbling, and the sound of a chair
being pushed back upon stones. A monk, in his black habit,
smiled a welcome. I suspect we had woken him from a
nap.

He spoke little English. We had no Greek, but he nodded
and smiled, and led the way across the courtyard to the chapel.
He was obviously very proud of it. His face was lined and
tired, I thought, although he could not have been much more
than forty, but it lit up with happiness as he conducted us from
one ikon to another and stood back to let us study them.

Truth to tell, the place was so dark, and the ikons so dimly lit that I am sure we saw less than half of the beauties with which he was familiar. But we admired them, and followed our guide on a further tour of inspection.

It was uncannily quiet. Our companion was the only living soul we saw. Could the other monks be away for the day, or locked somewhere in meditation or prayer? We did not like to enquire, and in any case could not possibly ask for enlightenment in the primitive sign language we were obliged to use for communication.

We followed him through a long room which reminded me so sharply of Fairacre's village hall that a pang of homesickness swept over me. Wooden chairs were ranged all round the walls. A billiard table took up the major part of the room, and photographs hung awry on the walls.

Everywhere lay dust. The smell of sea-damp clung about the rooms, and the banisters and rails were sticky with the all-pervading salty air.

Our host continued to smile and to point out objects of interest – a framed text, incomprehensible of course, to us, an archway, a window. At last we came back to the door where we had met him. What, we wondered, did we do about alms-giving? We noticed a wooden platter on a low shelf, just inside the door, in which a few coins lay. We put our own upon them, looking questioningly at our guide, who nodded and smiled and bowed.

He held our hands in farewell. His were cold and bony, and with a rare maternal urge I wished suddenly that I could cook him a luscious meal and build a good fire, to keep out the desolation of the place.

We retraced our steps. I was chilled to the marrow, and would have been glad to climb back into the car, but Amy strode across to a white marble war memorial hard by the deserted mill, and I followed her.

The monastery itself had been forlorn enough, but here was the very essence of sadness. Against the foot of the cross was propped a wreath of brown dead laurel leaves. Above it, the inscription was streaked with brown stains. Dead grass shuddered in the wind from the sea, and nearby an old fruit cage, its wire broken and rusty, protected nothing but a jungle of tall grass bleached white by the salt winds, and rustling like the wings of a flock of birds.

Another chapel stood beyond it. It too was deserted, some of the windows broken and boarded. On this magnificent headland, in its proud position as one of the bastions of Christianity, it was infinitely sad to see this once-loved, splendid place, so desolate and forlorn.

We returned in silence to the car, too moved to speak, until we had wound our way down the great hill and reached the road again.

This experience had made us pensive, and I reflected, as we drove in silence, upon the life of the monk, living in chill discomfort, in that remote place high above the sea. For once, my smugness at contemplating the single life was shaken. I felt again the touch of the cold thin hand in mine, the gritty dampness of the surrounding walls, the dust, the darkness.

And, for a moment, I looked upon a lot which might well be mine and other solitary old people's in the future, where loneliness and bleakness stalked, and even the light of religious beliefs could do little to comfort.

I shivered, and Amy patted my knee with a warm hand.

Thank God for friends, I thought gratefully.

*　　　*　　　*

Our spirits rose as we took a roundabout route back to the hotel. The clouds lifted, and the blue Cretan sky was above us again.

We stopped in Kritsa, a village we had grown to love, a few miles from our hotel. It lay in the hills among olive and carob groves, and there were wonderful walks nearby, as we had discovered.

We sat on a log on the side of the hill, our feet in the damp grass. In the distance we could see a woman on her balcony busy spinning wool on a hand spindle. Nearer at hand, another woman dragged branches of carob tree towards three splendid white goats, who strained at their chains bleating madly. Their stubby tails flickered with excitement and anticipation, and as soon as the greenstuff was near enough they fell upon it, crunching the bean pods with every appearance of delight.

We walked down the hill and revisited the church. This was freshly whitewashed, and as spruce inside as out. Two dark-eyed children jostled each other as they rushed towards us, a bunch of wilting flowers in their hands, hoping for custom.

There were two letters for me when we returned, which I welcomed with cries of joy. Why is it that letters when away are so much more satisfying than those that drop through one's own letter box?

One was from the kennels assuring me that Tibby had settled down well, was eating everything put before her, including the dried food which is spurned at home, and seemed well content.

How typical of a cat, I thought sourly. At home, she will reject anything from a tin, and all forms of dried cat food. Rabbit, from *China* not *Australia*, is welcomed, preferably still warm from her personal casserole, raw meat cut very

small, and occasionally poached fish. Her tastes are far too extravagant for a teacher's budget, but I weakly give in. Now, it seemed, she wolfed everything in sight, and made me appear an even bigger ass than I am.

The other letter was from Mrs Partridge, the vicar's wife, and I thought how uncommonly kind she was to take time from all her commitments to cover three pages to me with all the news of Fairacre.

Mrs Pringle's bad leg had flared up again and Dr Martin had been to see her. However, she was still at work, both in the school and the school house. (I could foresee that I should have to express my gratitude and admiration to the martyr, when I returned, in terms as fulsome as my conscience would

117

permit.) The Mawnes had held a coffee party which raised twenty-eight pounds, and would no doubt have raised more but it rained, which damped things. (Not surprising.)

Mr Mawne had high hopes of my returning with plenty of pictures of the hawk. Had I had any luck? The Coggs twins had gone down with measles, but appeared to be playing with all and sundry, as recommended by modern medical men – such a mistake; it would never have been allowed in their own nursery – so no doubt my numbers at school would be much depleted when term began.

She ended with high hopes for my complete recovery and kind regards to Amy.

'I am to pass on Mrs Partridge's kind regards,' I said, turning to her. She was engrossed in a letter of her own, and did not reply for a minute or two.

'Very sweet of her,' she remarked absently, looking up at last. She waved her own letter.

'From Vanessa. She wants a silk scarf trimmed with little gold discs. You can wear it over your head, she says, and somebody called Bobo, or maybe Baba – the child's handwriting is appalling – Dawson, brought one home from Greece recently and looks "fantastic" – spelt with a "k" – in it.'

Amy looked enquiringly at me.

'Have you seen such a thing?'

'There are lots in the hotel shop.'

'Must be white, black or a "yummy sort of raspberry pink",' said Amy, consulting the letter.

'I think I saw a black one.'

'Then we'll snap it up as soon as the shop opens,' said Amy decisively. 'I'm not trying to track down "a yummy sort of raspberry pink". By the way, Gerard's been up to Scotland again. It does look hopeful, doesn't it?'

'He's bound to be there quite a bit,' I pointed out reasonably, 'if he's doing this book on Scottish poets.'

Amy snorted.

'He's staying at Vanessa's hotel, and she sounds delighted to see him. I should say there's definitely something cooking there. Here, would you like to read her letter?'

'Read all about Fairacre in return,' I said, as we exchanged missives, and I settled back in the armchair to decipher Vanessa's sprawling hand. Amy certainly had the best of this bargain, I thought, remembering Mrs Partridge's immaculate copperplate.

'This Hattie May,' I said, struggling laboriously through the letter, 'she had tea with. Does she mean *the* Hattie May who was leading lady in all those musical comedies just after the war?'

'Must be, I suppose. She faded out after she married, I remember.'

'Well, Vanessa says that she is now a window – widow, presumably – and happily settled in a cottage near their hotel. I think I saw her in everything she did. What a dancer!'

'Come to think of it,' said Amy, putting down Mrs Partridge's letter, 'she mentioned her when she stayed with me last. Hattie May was living in the hotel then and looking for a permanent home. Nice of her to invite Vanessa out. I sometimes wonder if the child is lonely up there. Scotland always seems such an empty sort of country.'

'That's its attraction. Anyway, Gerard told you that there were lots of young men who were being attentive, and I can't imagine a stunning-looking female like Vanessa being short of companions.'

'You're probably right,' agreed Amy. 'And anyway, I imagine Gerard is to the forefront of the attentive ones. I hope he can persuade Vanessa to become a little more literate when they are married.'

'Amy!' I cried, 'you are quite incorrigible! Let's go and change.'

'And then,' said Amy, 'we must do Vanessa's shopping. I have a feeling I shall never be paid for it.'

We had a splendid dinner, as usual, with lamb cooked in a particularly succulent sauce made with the magnificent Cretan tomatoes and a touch of garlic. Afterwards we pottered round the shop and Amy bought a black scarf for Vanessa and some silver pendants for presents.

My purchases were more modest and consisted of attractive tiles which I hoped would be acceptable to Mrs Pringle and other kind souls who had made the holiday possible. Amy was admiring one of the beautiful gold plaited belts, and resisting temptation with remarkable strength of will. They were certainly expensive, and I hoped that she would not weaken and buy one, as I fully intended to get her one myself as a little thank-offering for her generosity over the past few weeks.

She left the belts reluctantly, and we returned to our little house with our purchases. The moon was out, and the night was calm.

We went out and descended the steps through the sweet-smelling night air. The scent of the lilies hung heavily about us. We walked in amicable silence along the sea-shore. Little waves splashed and sucked at the sand, and a flickering silvery pathway lay across the sea to the moon. It was one of those moments I should remember for the rest of my life, I knew.

We were in bed early that night, and Amy was asleep long before I was. Somehow, sleep evaded me. I could not get the memory of Toplou from my mind. That deserted place, with the wind crying in its courtyards, haunted me. And the tired patient face of the monk, so gently smiling and polite, floated before me in the moonlight. He seemed to embody the spirit of his surroundings, the lost splendour and the forgotten ardour.

The experience had shaken me, for it had presented me with the stark surprising fact that single people can be lonely. My own solitary state had always been a source of some secret pride to me. I was independent. I could do as I liked. Now I had seen the other side of the coin, and I found it daunting.

All my old night-time fears came flocking back. Suppose my health gave way? Suppose I out-lived all my friends? And why didn't I set about buying a little house *now*, instead of shelving the idea? Someone else, all too soon, would need the school house when they took over my post. I must start facing things, or the bleakness of the monk's life would be echoed in mine.

Perhaps Amy was right to be so engrossed in match-making. Crippled though she was, at the moment, by the blows to her own marriage, maybe she was being true to a proper urge, something natural and normal, when she took such a keen interest in Vanessa's future. Some inner wisdom, as old as mankind itself, stirred Amy's endeavours. Maybe, in my comfortable arrogance, I was missing more than I cared to admit.

I thought how smug I had been when married friends had

told me of their problems; how perfunctorily for instance, I had disposed of Mrs Clark's dilemma. The truth was, I told myself severely, that, as in all things, celibacy has its good and bad sides. Nine times out of ten I was happy with my lot, which was as it should be. If I have to live by myself, it is as well to be on good terms with myself.

On the other hand, this salutary jolt would do me no harm. Toplou had made me suddenly aware, not only of the sadness of the solitary, but the warmth of loving companionship, which Amy had spoken of so movingly, which marriage can bring.

The dawn was flushing the sky with rose, and the small birds were twittering among the orange trees, before I finally fell asleep.

12 The Last Day

THE last day of our holiday arrived much too quickly.
My feelings were divided. On one side, I hated the idea
of leaving this lovely place, probably for ever, for I
doubted if I should be able to come again. On the other hand,
the thought of going home to the waiting house and garden,
to wicked Tibby and to all my Fairacre friends was wonderfully elating. I remembered Amy's amusement at my excitement on returning home from Bent. But surely wasn't that as
it should be? How dreadful life would be if home were not the
best place in it.

We decided to potter about the town and hotel rather than
make a long excursion. We were to start at the gruelling time
of five-thirty the next morning, catching an aeroplane from
Heraklion a little before eight. If all went well, we should be
home about tea-time.

After breakfast, Amy drove the car back to the garage from
which we had hired it, and I was left to my own devices. The
first thing I did was to hurry to the shop and select the finest
gold belt available, taking advantage of Amy's absence.

Having secreted it among my pile of packing, I took my
camera and set out on a last-minute filming expedition. A small
private boatyard adjoined the hotel, and here I had been
watching a young couple painting their boat in white and blue,
with here and there a touch of scarlet. It was most attractive,

and, with the blue sea and sky beyond it, would make a perfect colour photograph.

Then there were close-ups of some of the exotic flowers to take. I might have fallen down badly on Mr Mawne's Cretan hawk, but I intended to have something noteworthy to show the Women's Institute at some future meeting in Fairacre's village hall.

I was hailed by a voice as I passed the Clarks' house. Mrs Clark was sunning herself on the verandah.

'Are you off today?'

I said we were, unfortunately.

'We're staying another week. Do come and sit down. John has walked down to the town to get the newspapers.'

I sank into a deckchair and closed my eyes against the dazzling sunshine.

'I wonder if I shall ever feel sun as hot as this again at ten-thirty in the morning.'

'Of course you will. I've no doubt you'll come again next year, or sometime before long.'

'And what about you?'

'More hopeful, my dear. We are staying on this extra week for the express purpose of looking for something to rent, probably for a few months next winter.'

'So you are still thinking of coming here to live?'

Mrs Clark's expression became a trifle grim.

'John is. He found the most appalling house in Malia. Far too big, needing three servants at least, and crumbling into the bargain. I can't make him realise that, if I do agree to come, we simply must have something we can manage on our own. We shall be far from rich on an army pension, and John still seems to imagine we shall have batmen hovering round us. I've persuaded him to try a short period here before we do anything drastic. I must say, he's agreed very readily.'

'It seems sensible,' I said.

'Well, we have to adapt, otherwise marriage could be a very uncomfortable state.'

She shifted her chair so that her face was in the shade. Her legs, I noticed, were a far more beautiful shade of brown than my own.

'Have you read *Mansfield Park*?' she asked unexpectedly.

'Constantly.'

'Do you remember a passage near the beginning when the Crawfords discuss matrimony? Mary Crawford says something to the effect that we are all apt to expect too much, "but then, if one scheme of happiness fails, human nature turns to another – we find comfort somewhere." I often think of that. It's very true, and no marriage will work unless there is a willingness to adapt a little. I've no doubt we'll end very comfortably, one way or the other. The danger is in making long-term decisions too quickly, and I'm glad that I've made John see that.'

She sighed, and wriggled her bare toes in the sunshine.

'Why I should worry you with my affairs, I can't think. It's that sympathetic face of yours, you know.'

There was the sound of footsteps on the path, and John appeared with the newspapers.

'I must go,' I said, after we had exchanged greetings. 'I'm off to take photographs of all the things I meant to take days ago. I shall see you again before we go.'

I left them together, John in my vacated chair. They were smiling at each other.

Plenty of give-and-take there, I thought, going on my way. But I hoped she would win.

We had our last lunch at a favourite restaurant nearby. Here the shrimps seemed to be larger than ever, the salads even more delicious. Two cats attended us, and obligingly cleared up the shrimps' heads and tails. Would Tibby have been so helpful? Perhaps, after her Spartan fare at the kennels . . .

We sauntered back, replete, to the welcome shade ot our little house, and lay on our beds to rest. Outside, the light and heat beat from the white walls. All was quiet, wrapped in the hush of siesta time. Only the sea moved, splashing its minute waves on the beach below us.

'Must remember to put out my air-sick pills,' yawned Amy. 'That's the thing to take shares in, you know. Wholesale chemists. When you think of the handfuls of pills the G.Ps hand out these days, you can't go wrong.'

'I'll remember,' I said, 'when I don't know what to do with my spare cash.'

'My Aunt Minnie,' went on Amy languidly, 'left me some hundreds of shares in something called Nicaraguan Railways or Peruvian Copper. I can't quite recall the name, but something far-flung in the general direction of South America. They bring in a dividend of about thirty-five pence every half year. James says for pity's sake sell 'em, but I don't like to. She was a dear old thing, though addicted to musical evenings, and she left me a beautiful ring.'

'The one you're wearing?'

Amy has a square-cut emerald which is my idea of a perfect ring.

'No. This is part of the product of five hideous rings my

dear mother left me. She was left four of them by her older sisters, and every one was the same setting – a row of five diamonds like a tiny sparkling set of false teeth. I sold them when she died, and bought this instead, and put the rest in the Caxley Building Society. Very useful that money has been too, for this and that.'

Silence fell. It was very hot, even in our stone-built house, but I gloried in it. How long before I saw sunshine like this again, I wondered? Amy's eyes were closed, and I was beginning to plan my packing when she spoke again.

'Did you have musical evenings when you were young? Aunt Minnie's were real shockers, especially as she made me accompany the singers, who were no keener on my assistance than I was on their efforts. She had a baby grand, covered with a horrible eastern scarf thing, ornamented with bits of looking-glass, and *nothing* would persuade her to open the lid. Mind you, it would have been a day's work to clear off all the silver-framed photographs, not to mention the arrangement of dried grasses. We all just soldiered on, while Aunt Minnie nodded her head, and tapped her foot in approximate time to the music.'

'We got stuck with oratorios mainly,' I remembered. ' "Penitence, Pardon and Peace", "Olivet to Calvary", "The Crucifixion". My father could sing very well. Unfortunately, I couldn't play very well. Tempers used to get rather frayed, until we fell back on something simpler, like "The Lost Chord" or "Merry Goes The Time When The Heart Is Young".'

'I sometimes think,' said Amy, 'that people of our generation who are constantly mourning "the good old days" must have forgotten such things as musical evenings, and starched knickers, and washdays tackled with yellow soap and a wash-board.'

'And button-hooks that pinched your flesh, and elastic driving you mad under your chin,' I added. 'Children have such lovely clothes these days. No wonder they learn to dress themselves so much earlier than we did.'

'A case of have to, I expect, with all the mums having to rush off to work.'

Amy grunted contentedly and turned her face into the pillow. Peace descended again, and I lay listening to the gentle splashing of the waves and the chirruping of a nearby cricket until I too drifted into sleep.

We slept for over an hour and woke much refreshed.

'Let's ring for tea here,' suggested Amy, 'and remind them about early breakfast. What hopes of bread rolls, I wonder?'

It had been a standing joke. Each morning our tray had arrived with one bread roll each, a sweetish confection rather like a Bath bun without the sugar, and a slice of sultana cake. Accompanying these things was a small dish of unidentifiable jam.

The bread rolls were excellent. The other things too cloying for our taste first thing in the morning. Marmalade we had on one unforgettable occasion. Our telephone conversation with the kitchen staff ran on the same lines each morning.

'Hello. This is room twenty eight.'

''Ullo. Good morning. Breakfast?'

'Please, for two. Coffee for two.'

'Coffee for two.'

'Bread rolls for two. NO BUNS OR CAKE, PLEASE.'

'Bread rolls. No ozzer zings?'

'No, thanks. Just bread rolls.'

'Just blead rolls.'

'And *marmalade*, please, not jam.'

'Just marmalade. No nice jam?'

'No, thanks.'

'Bleakfast coming.'

'Thank you.'

'Okay. You're welcome.'

And within a few minutes the waiter would arrive with a beaming smile, and a few words of English, and a laden tray with exactly the same food as before.

'We might just as well save our breath,' Amy had said. But I disagreed. It was part of the fun to keep trying, and as I pointed out, we had been given marmalade *once*.

I must say it seemed odd that with oranges and lemons bowing the trees to the ground with the weight of their fruit, marmalade seemed to be looked upon as a luxury. As it was, we had been obliged to buy a jar in the town, and very poor stuff it was, reminding me of the jam manufacturer who made a fortune from his product SPINRUT, the main ingredient of which can be readily recognised by those who can read backwards.

Our tea tray arrived, and we were told that, as we had to make such an early start, our breakfast would be delivered in the evening, with the coffee in a flask. We received the news stoically, as befitted Britishers.

'At least it will wash down the Kwells,' Amy pointed out. 'Let's go out and get some air.'

It was still too hot for much exertion, but we strolled in the shade of the trees, and watched the more energetic holiday-makers swimming in the pool. A gardener was pushing a hand

mower very carefully and slowly over the two tiny lawns. The hose and sprinkler lay nearby. I wished my lawn at Fairacre received such love. It would be the showpiece of the village. It was sad to think that this time tomorrow I should not be here to see the sprinkler at work on those two thirsty patches.

Later, after dinner, we took a last walk through the streets of Aghios Nikolaos, and stopped for coffee at our favourite café.

The night was velvety dark, and we sat at a table near the water's edge. The sea slapped the bottoms of the moored boats as they swayed at anchor. Out to sea, a lighted ferry boat chugged across to Piraeus, and I wished that one day I might visit Greece itself.

As though reading my thoughts, Amy said: 'We haven't seen nearly enough, of course. Next time we must stop in Athens, and then come on to Crete and see the western end. The thing to do would be to spend six months or a year in these parts.'

'I can't see our Education Committee giving me leave of absence for that time,' I observed.

'If things don't turn out well at home,' said Amy slowly, 'it's a comfort to think there's so much to do here. I shall hang on to the idea. It would be a life-line to sanity, wouldn't it? I mean, in the presence of civilisations as old as these, one's own troubles seem pretty insignificant. Or so I've found, anyway,' she added, 'during the past fortnight.'

'I'm more glad than I can say, to hear you say that,' I told her soberly.

'And I can't thank you enough for coming with me. You've been the perfect companion for an old misery like me.'

'*Thank me*?' I cried. 'Why, it's entirely – '

But Amy cut me short.

'One word of thanks from you, my dear, and I shall throw those sandals you've just kicked off, into the sea, and you'll have to walk back to the hotel barefoot!'

The threat sufficed. Amy had won, as usual. We took our time over the coffee, and lingered to look at the sea on our way home.

Sure enough, on the low table in our room the breakfast tray waited for us. It was covered with a snowy cloth.

When we came to investigate we found one bread roll, one bun, one slice of cake and a dish of dark brown (fig?) jam apiece. Two stout flasks flanked our empty cups.

'Well, there we are,' said Amy, replacing the cloth. 'How

about that at five in the morning? I don't think I'll be able to face a thing.'

'I shall,' I said robustly. 'Just think how far it is to England! Why, we may not be able to eat on the plane.'

'I shan't want to,' replied Amy, putting her Kwells on the tray, with a sigh.

We undressed and climbed into our beds for the last time. I meant to lie awake for a little, savouring all the pleasures of scent and sound that came drifting from the garden at night, but I scarcely had time to arrange my pillow before sleep overcame me, and a few minutes after that, it seemed, the telephone was trilling, telling us to get up in readiness for our departure.

13 Going Home

IT was still dark when we set off along the bumpy road to Heraklion, but by the time we were in the aeroplane, the sky was filled with rows of little pink clouds, made glorious by the sunrise.

We circled the island, and I wondered, with a pang, if I should ever set foot there again. The experience had opened my eyes to a larger, more beautiful world, to an ancient culture happier than our own, and had given me a glimpse of 'the glory that was Greece.'

I felt wonderfully refreshed, and my arm and ankle were so much better that I discarded my sling whenever possible. Prudence, however, made me wear it on the flight. One gets jostled quite badly enough during travel when hale and hearty. With a slowly-knitting bone, I intended to take all precautions.

We made an unscheduled stop at Athens. The workmen were still pushing screaming machines over the marble floor, and the dust was as thick as ever. However, we found a cup of good coffee and a very nasty chocolate biscuit apiece, while we waited, and then we were herded aboard the new aeroplane.

Amy had taken her Kwells, with a swig of flask coffee and much shuddering, and dozed for most of the journey. I had insisted that she sat by the window this time, so that I was in the middle seat of the three. There were a good many empty seats, so that I was somewhat surprised when a lone female came to sit by me.

'Haven't I seen you in Aghios Nikolaos?' she began.

I said indeed she might have done.

'I saw your friend had dropped off, and thought you might be glad of some company,' she said.

'How kind of you.'

'Well, I'm a schoolteacher, and I should think you are too, so I thought we might have something in common.'

Now, I am not ashamed of being a schoolteacher, rather the reverse, when I consider that I am still strong and healthy after so many years of classroom battling, but there is something depressing in being told that one wears one's profession like a brand upon one's forehead – the mark of the beast, in fact.

I said civilly that yes, I was a schoolteacher.

'There's a look, isn't there?' she prattled.

'Downtrodden? Hungry? Mad?'

'Not quite that. Shabby perhaps, and not much given to dressing well and making-up properly.'

This was really rather hard. I had visited the hairdresser at the hotel the night before, and she had given her all. Never had I looked so *bouffant*, so glossy, so truly feminine. The sunshine had produced high-lights which I had never before seen in my normal mouse, and I was looking forward to dazzling Fairacre with my new glamour, and my suntan.

I was also wearing an expensive – for me – pale pink linen dress and jacket, and Aunt Clara's seed pearls, not to mention new white sandals. And here was this stranger, bursting in upon my previous solitude, and generally undermining my self-confidence.

I was catty enough to notice her own crumpled floral print

frock and dirty white cardigan, and also her undistinguished coiffure, but was humane enough to forbear to comment. Really, civility puts almost too great a strain on mankind at times.

Primitive woman, I reflected, under such provocation, would have torn the greasy hair from this person's head in handfuls, and felt very much better for the exercise.

Instead, I asked her where she had stayed in Aghios Nikolaos and she mentioned a hotel near our own, which we had visited for lunch once.

'If I'd had the money,' she said, 'I should have stayed where you were, but you can't do that on a teacher's salary.'

She sounded suspicious, and I wondered if she thought I had some secret source of income – heroin, perhaps, smuggled in the heels of my new shoes. Obviously, in her eyes, my age and dowdy appearance would exonerate me from any other immoral activity.

I did not rise to the bait, but asked her if she had far to go when we reached Heathrow, and she told me that she lived at Chatham near the docks, and would be met by her fiancé and his twin brother. They were *exactly* alike, and went everywhere together.

I asked when she hoped to get married, and wondered, but didn't ask, if both twins would be together on the honeymoon.

'Next Easter,' she said, and went on to ask where I lived. I told her.

'It's so pretty round there,' she said enthusiastically. I agreed.

'You wouldn't like to exchange houses, I suppose? It sounds a lovely place for a honeymoon, and Chatham would make a nice change for you.'

'Frankly, no. I seldom leave home,' I said shortly.

I put one of my magazines firmly upon her knee, and opened my own.

She looked aggrieved, but opened it obediently, and silence fell.

I glanced at comatose Amy. One eye opened and shut again in a conspiratorial wink. Amy doesn't miss much.

A few minutes later she roused herself, and sat up with a yawn.

'What a lovely nap! What's the time?'

The stranger told her, returned my magazine and stood up.

'I'll go back to my seat now,' she said, showing more tact than I imagined she had. On the other hand, it was said so primly, that maybe she had taken offence at my disobliging refusal to exchange houses. Whatever the reason, it was a great relief to see her depart, after such an unnerving encounter in mid-air.

We were late arriving at Heathrow and we seemed to wait for hours around the revolving contraption that disgorges one's luggage. Why is it, I wondered, that other people's luggage always seems superior in size, quality and polish to one's own? I was somewhat cheered by watching a red-faced man, very much like our local farmer Mr Roberts, collecting his pieces of battered luggage, each securely lashed with orange binder twine.

'I've lost two good leather straps up here in my time,' he said, catching my eye. 'They won't bother with binder twine, and if they do there's plenty more where that came from.'

Amy rang the garage whilst I collected our bags, and hours later, it seemed, we settled ourselves into her car.

The air was chilly, the clouds like a grey tent, low over us.

Rain lashed the tarmac, umbrellas glistened all around, and goose-pimples stood on our arms. One could almost feel the tan fading.

We were in England again.

'What an extraordinary woman that was,' commented Amy, as we drove from the airport. 'I noticed her once or twice when we were walking about the town. She seemed to be holidaying alone.'

'I'm not surprised.'

'A typical case of someone who lives alone,' continued Amy, hooting at the motorist in front of us who had signalled that he was going left for the last half-mile, then right, and eventually went straight on.

'How do you mean?'

'Well, there's a tendency for solitary people – *some* of them, I should say – to tag on to complete strangers and engage them in conversation. Lonely, of course, that's all, but a trifle disconcerting for those button-holed. And then these loners never stop talking. Most exhausting. I must say, you choked off that poor dear in a brutally efficient way.'

I began to feel qualms on two counts.

'I hope I wasn't brutal,' I said.

'Let's say *decisive*,' said Amy, 'and I really don't blame you after such cheek on her part.'

'And I hope I don't waylay people and talk too much,' I added, expressing my second fear.

Amy laughed indulgently.

'You silly old dear! You've always talked too much!'

I digested this unpalatable truth as we drove towards Bent. We had arranged to go straight to Amy's house from Heathrow, when we planned the holiday. It was nearer than Fairacre, and we both felt that a good night's sleep after our flight would enable us to face the home chores before us.

As always, Amy's house presented a calm and beautiful aspect. There were flowers in every room, no sign of dust, everything immaculate and welcoming. There was even a tray laid ready for two complete with biscuit tin, and Amy lost no time in putting on the kettle.

A pile of letters stood on the hall table, and Amy looked at it anxiously as we brought in her luggage from the car.

'I'll tackle that later,' she said.

I was in my old bedroom overlooking the corn fields. In the driving rain nothing was moving. No doubt the farmers were cursing all around, I thought, for some of the fields I could see were only half-cut.

But despite the rain, my spirits were high. We were home again, back among the wet fields, the dripping trees, the little runnels of brown rainwater chattering along the roadside. I thought of those two parched lawns at the hotel, as I gazed at Amy's lush slopes before me. A thrush, head cocked on one side, was listening for a worm, and three sparrows searched among the plants in the border, with raindrops splashing on their little tabby backs. Somewhere, far away, a sheep bleated, and another answered it. The fragrance of wet earth and leaves was everywhere, and I thanked heaven for the sights and scents of home.

Later that evening, Amy read her correspondence, sorting it into piles very tidily, while I read a gardening magazine and learnt about all the things I should have done last spring in order to have a flourishing flower border next season.

'Too late,' I said aloud.

'What is?'

'Taking pipings and cuttings, and sowing seeds ready for planting out this autumn, and a hundred other things. It's an extraordinary thing, but whenever I rush to the nurseryman in autumn, fired to have some particular plant, then the right time to put it in was last spring. And, of course, when I rush there in the spring, the particular plants I'm mad for should have gone in last autumn.'

'I must remember to give you a basic gardening book for Christmas,' said Amy severely. 'You sound the most haphazard gardener. It's a wonder yours looks as well as it does. Mr Willet, I suppose?'

She patted her piles of correspondence into neat stacks.

'Friends who won't mind waiting. Friends who will mind waiting. Business and bills,' she said, surveying them.

'Well, bills could go on the won't-mind-waiting stack, I should think.'

Amy shook her head.

'I was brought up as you were, my dear, to pay as I went along. I've a perfect horror of owing money, born of a frugal upbringing. As for hire purchase, my blood runs cold at the thought. Suppose I suddenly had no money – '

She stopped, and looked out at the grey evening. When she spoke again, her voice had altered.

'A letter from James among this lot.' It was in the friends-who-will-mind-waiting pile, I noticed. 'He's still pressing for a divorce. What a hopeless situation this is! I wonder what the outcome will be? I felt so strong and sensible while we were away, but now I'm back I feel as wobbly as a jellyfish.'

'Put it out of your mind,' I advised. 'You've had a long day

travelling. Things will seem saner after a night's sleep. And if I were you,' I added, 'I should transfer his letter to the friends-who-*won't*-mind-waiting pile.'

Amy laughed, and did so. It seemed to give her some comfort.

Next morning the sky was blue, and our breakfast table was bathed in sunshine. I presented Amy with the plaited gold belt, with which she was agreeably delighted. Beside my plate was a large square parcel which turned out to contain a splendid book of photographs of Crete with short accounts of the different places. It was a perfect memento of a perfect holiday.

We drove back to Fairacre by way of the kennels, where

Tibby sat on top of her sleeping house, looking aloof. I stroked her head, and muttered endearments to which she responded with a yawn.

Only when she was safely in the car, secured in the cat basket, did she deign to give tongue, and then only to keep up the nerve-racking caterwauling by which she registers strong disapproval of car travel.

'I hope you've got a supply of the tenderer portions of the most expensive rabbit,' shouted Amy, above the din.

'It's "Pussi-luv" or nothing,' I shouted back. 'If she can eat it in the kennels, she can eat it at home.'

We turned into the school lane. My hedge seemed to have grown six inches in the past fortnight, and the lawn needed cutting. But the border was full of colour, despite my abortive forays to the nurseryman.

I felt under the third stone on the right of the porch, and withdrew the key. The door was difficult to open, because there was a pile of letters still on the mat. One was stuck in the letter box.

It was a note in Mrs Partridge's handwriting, and I put it aside to read later. Probably, a change of date for the W.I., I thought.

We picked up the letters and put them on the hall table. Tibby was released, and bounded into the garden, giving us time to look around us.

Something was wrong. The house smelt musty. Everything was tidy, but a fine layer of dust was everywhere. Unlike Amy's house, there were no flowers. Usually, Mrs Pringle does me proud with a handful of marigolds stuffed in a mug, but today there was nothing.

'Come and sit down,' I said to Amy. 'This is all very

strange. Something must have happened to Mrs P. There may be a note in the kitchen.'

But there was no note. The paint had been washed, the windows cleaned, the sink whitened with bleach, the dish-cloth draped along its edge, stiff and dry, but here too, dust lay.

I filled the kettle for coffee, remembered Mrs Partridge's note, and read it while the kettle boiled.

It said:

So sorry to tell you that Mrs Pringle is in hospital – probably appendicitis, nothing very serious, but she was worried because she could not get in the last-minute provisions.

If you are not too tired, do have dinner with us tonight. Very simple. About 7.30. Longing to hear about Crete.

Cordelia Partridge

I handed it to Amy, and set about putting out the cups. I was sincerely sorry for my old sparring partner in hospital, and remembered how kind she had been to me at the beginning of the holiday when I had had my accident.

'Poor old girl,' I said, spooning instant coffee into the cups. 'I must ring the hospital later on. I suppose she'll be at Caxley.'

'I expect all this "bottoming" brought it on,' said Amy, gazing at my dazzling paintwork.

'Don't rub salt in my wounds,' I begged her. 'I'm already suffering from remorse for all the things I've said to her in my time.'

'She can take it,' said Amy robustly. 'And anyway, she gives as good as she gets, from all I hear.'

She finished her coffee, and stood up.

'Must be off. Dozens of things to do at Bent, and you have just as many here, I can see.'

I waved goodbye to her, watching until the car turned the bend in the lane, and went back to the garden.

My new rose bush had a dozen or more coppery buds on it, and the lavender hedge was in full flower. A few bumble bees buzzed lazily among the blossoms, and Tibby approached and weaved herself round my legs affectionately.

I picked up the exasperating animal and gave her a hug.

'Tibby,' I told her. 'We're really home!'

Part Three

Return to Fairacre

14 Mrs Pringle Falls Ill

THERE is no doubt about it, going away does one so much good because, for one thing, it makes one's home seem doubly desirable.

I pondered on this truth as I walked round to the vicarage under my umbrella. The hotel could not be faulted, but how much cosier the small rooms of the school house seemed, and what a blessing it was to drink cold water straight from the tap, instead of having tepid mineral water, tasting faintly of soda, from a bottle!

And how green everything was! I looked with approval at the glistening hedges, the flowers drenched with rain, and the great green flanks of the downs where the sheep were grazing. I even felt kindly towards a worm which was struggling on Mrs Partridge's doorstep, and transferred it to a luscious wet garden bed. There had been no worms in Crete.

'Come in! Come in!' cried the vicar, and to my surprise he clasped me close to his Donegal tweed jacket, and kissed me on both cheeks. I felt as though I had returned from some long exile in the salt-mines.

'My dear, she's come!' he announced, ushering me into the drawing room where Mrs Partridge sat knitting.

'Bootees,' she said, after we had exchanged greetings and I had been supplied with a glass of sherry. 'For the sale, dear, but I've made a most unfortunate mistake. Can you see?'

Certainly, there was something strangely awry with the garment.

'I think you've knitted a row or two with a piece of wool that was hanging down, and not the main line, if you follow me.'

'Oh dear, it's these glasses! I've mislaid my others. They're bound to turn up, they always do. Last time they were in the laundry book. So I'm driven to wearing these.'

'Shall I undo it for you?'

Mrs Partridge looked anguished.

'*Must you*? Shall we put it aside for a bit, and just enjoy our drinks?'

We did so, and I answered a volley of questions about the holiday, until I could ask about Mrs Pringle.

'I did try to ring the hospital,' I said. 'Three times, but the exchange didn't answer.'

'I know. What has happened to all those nice girls who used to be so obliging years ago, I simply don't know. I can remember, many a time, asking for a number and the girl would say: "If it's Mrs Henry you want, I'm afraid she's out shopping. I saw her go into Boots not five minutes ago." So friendly, and always had time to let you know about their families. Gerald used to find them such a help when people needed visiting.'

'Those days have gone,' I agreed. 'I suppose it would be all the same if one were lying with two broken legs and a fire in the house, though no doubt 999 might answer.'

Mrs Partridge nodded thoughtfully.

'Except that you would not be able to get to the phone with two broken legs, and the fire might be your side of it.'

'Tell me about Mrs Pringle,' I said. One can't afford to be too literal.

It appeared that she was taken ill in Caxley on market day.

'In Woolworth's, and I must say the manager sounds a thoroughly sensible fellow and deserves promotion, for he fetched a doctor, and she was taken straight to Caxley hospital.'

The Vicar intervened.

'Don't tell her what they found, my dear,' he advised his wife. 'We are eating soon.'

I was grateful to him. He knows of my squeamishness.

Mrs Partridge looked disappointed, but loyally kept to generalities.

'Top and bottom of it was that they operated within an hour or two, and she'll be there for another week at least. But nothing serious. In fact, the hospital sister said she was comfortable when I enquired. It seemed a funny way to describe it when I know for a fact she was slit – '

'*Cordelia!*' said the vicar warningly.

'Sorry, sorry! Well, anyway, poor Mr Pringle had to go in, of course, taking nighties and things, and brought back the shopping, and was too upset to unpack it until next day. So the fish, my dear, from that jolly fellow in the market, was absolutely uneatable, and the cat was furious, Mrs Willet told me. You see, it *knows* it has fish on Thursdays.'

'Do you think our dinner is ready?' enquired the vicar.

'Of course it is. Come along,' said Mrs Partridge rising from the web of knitting wool criss-crossing the armchair.

'Cold chicken and salad,' she said, leading the way. 'I did warn you it would be simple, but I wish now I'd put some soup to heat. It's such a miserable evening for a cold meal. Shall I do that?'

We dissuaded her, protesting that cold chicken and salad would be splendid, and entered the dining room.

The meal was delicious, and afterwards, back in the drawing room, with the bootee growing even more grotesque, I caught up with the Fairacre news. Measles, it seemed, was now rife, and Mr Roberts' cowman had gone down with it and was in a very bad way.

'Of course, it will have its brighter side for you,' said Mrs Partridge. 'There won't be so many children next term, which will be a help with Mrs Pringle laid up.'

'I suppose I'd better look for someone else to stand in.'

'Well, Minnie Pringle won't be able to come. There's a new baby due, any minute now.'

'That's a relief. I shan't feel obliged to ask her. After ten minutes of Minnie's company, I'm nearly as demented as she is.'

'If the worst comes to the worst,' said the vicar, 'the older children must just turn to and help with the cleaning. Do it yourself, you know,' he added, beaming with pride at being so up-to-the-minute.

Mr and Mrs Mawne, it appeared, were in Scotland for a holiday, and I felt somewhat relieved. It would give me a breathing space before having to confess that I had no photographs of the Cretan hawk. The new people at Tyler's Row were repainting their house. Miss Waters' bad leg was responding to Dr Martin's liniment, and her sister had offered to embroider a new altar cloth.

At this stage, an enormous yawn engulfed me, which I did my best to hide, without success.

'It's time you were in bed,' said Mrs Partridge, looking over the top of the blameworthy glasses. 'You've had two busy days.'

It was true that I was almost asleep, but I did my best to look vivacious as I thanked her for a truly lovely evening, and departed into the rain.

Some poor baby, I thought, as I tottered home, was going to have a very odd bootee. Ah well, we all have to come to terms with life's imperfections, and one may as well begin young.

As might be expected, the minute I climbed into bed sleep eluded me, and I lay awake thinking about possible substitutes for Mrs Pringle, without success. I was going to visit her the next day, and hoped that she might have someone in mind. Otherwise, it looked as though the vicar's suggestion might have to be put into action.

After two hours or so of fruitless worrying, I heard St Patrick's clock chime, and then one solitary stroke. Very soon after this I must have fallen asleep, for I had a vivid dream in which the vicar was officiating at a marriage ceremony, clad in an improbable pale blue surplice. The bride was my importunate friend on the flight from Crete, and the groom was the monk from Toplou. Neither appeared to be interested in the ceremony, but were engrossed in a chess set which was lodged on the font.

I wonder what a psychiatrist would make of this?

The next morning I rang the hospital to enquire after my school cleaner. Mrs Pringle, I was not surprised to learn, was comfortable, and would be ready to receive visitors between two and four in the afternoon.

This was my first attempt at driving since the accident, and I was mightily relieved to find that I could do all that was necessary with my arm and foot.

Mrs Pringle, regal among her pillows, greeted me with

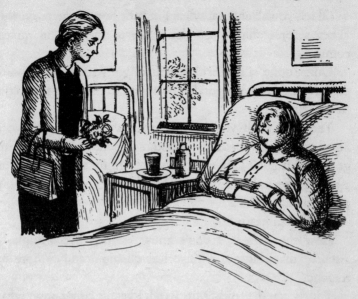

unaccustomed warmth, and admired the roses I had cut for her.

'A good thing I was handy for the hospital when it happened,' she told me. 'If I'd been slaving away at your place with nobody to call upon, I doubt if I'd be alive to tell the tale.'

I expressed my concern, and took the opportunity of thanking her for all the hard work she had put in at the school house, but I don't think she heard. Her mind was too full of more recent events.

'Ready to burst!' she told me with relish. 'Ready to burst! A mercy I didn't have to be jolted all the way to the County. I'd never have lasted out.'

She looked around her. Patients in neighbouring beds had fallen silent and were presumably listening to the saga. Mrs Pringle lowered her voice to a conspiratorial whisper.

'I'll tell you all about it when I'm back home,' she promised. 'There's some things you don't like to mention in mixed company.'

'Quite, quite,' I said briskly, thanking my stars for the postponement. It seemed a good opportunity to ask when she might be back in Fairacre.

'They don't tell you nothing here,' she grumbled. 'But I heard one of the nurses say something about next week, if all goes well. It don't look as though I'll be fit for school work for a bit. I've been thinking about it, and you know our Minnie's expecting again?'

I said I had heard.

'How she does it, I don't know,' sighed Mrs Pringle. I assumed that this was a rhetorical question, and forbore to respond.

'To tell you the truth, Miss Read, I've lost count now, what with his first family, and hers out of wedlock, and then these others. Then of course his eldest two are married and having families of their own. When I visit there – which isn't often I'm glad to say – there are babies all over the place, and I'm hard put to it to say whose are whose. Sometimes I wonder if Minnie knows herself.'

'No other ideas, I suppose?'

'There's Pringle's young brother, if you're really driven to it. He's quite handy at housework, but of course he'd have to come out from Caxley on the bus, and he's a bit simple. Nothing violent, I don't mean, but you'd have to watch your handbag and the dinner money.'

'It would be better to get someone in the village,' I said hastily, 'if we can find one.'

'There's no one,' said Mrs Pringle flatly, 'and we both knows it. How many wants housework these days? And specially school cleaning! Thankless job, that is, everlasting cleaning up after dozens of muddy boots. I sometimes think I must be soft in the head to keep the job on.'

Mrs Pringle's face was assuming its usual look of disgruntled self-pity, and I felt it was time to go.

'You're a marvel,' I told her, 'and keep the school beautifully. You deserve a good rest. We'll find someone, you'll see, and if the worst comes to the worst we shall have to do as the vicar suggested.'

'What's that?' asked Mrs Pringle suspiciously, on guard at once.

'Do it ourselves.'

'God help us!' cried Mrs Pringle, rolling her eyes heavenwards.

I made my farewells rapidly, before she had a total relapse.

Mr Willet turned up in the evening to cut the grass.

'I meant to have it all ship-shape for you when you got back,' he apologised, 'but what with the rain, and choir practice, and giving the Hales a hand with their outside painting when the rain let up – well, I never got round to it.'

I assured him that all was forgiven.

'That chap Hale,' he went on, 'got degrees and that, and a real nice bloke for a schoolmaster, but to see him with a paint brush is enough to make your hair curl! Paint all down the handle, paint all down his arm, drippin' off of his elbow – I tell you, he gets more on hisself than the woodwork! You could do out the Village Hall with what he wastes.'

He paused for breath.

'And how's the old girl?' he enquired, when he had recovered it. 'Still laughing fit to split?'

I said she seemed pretty bobbish, and told him about the dearth of supplementary school cleaners.

Mr Willet grew thoughtful.

'One thing, she did the place all through before she was took bad. I reckons we can keep it up together till she's fit again. After all, we shouldn't need to light them ruddy stoves she sets such store by. They're the main trouble. Won't hurt some of the bigger kids to lend a hand.'

'That's what the vicar said.'

'Ah!' nodded Mr Willet, setting off to fetch the lawn mower, 'and he said right too! Our Mr Partridge ain't such a fool as he looks.'

A minute later he wheeled out the mower. Above the clatter I heard him in full voice.

He was singing:

> *God moves in a mysterious way,*
> *His wonders to perform.*

15 Term Begins

AS always, the last week of the school holidays flew by with disconcerting speed. I had time to put the garden to rights, and to do a little shopping, but a great many other things, mainly school affairs, were shelved.

Nevertheless, I found time to call on Mrs Pringle, now at home and convalescent, and discovered, as we had all thought, that it would be two or three weeks before the doctor would allow her to resume work.

There was simply no one to be found who could take on her job, even temporarily. A fine look-out, I told myself, for the future, when Mrs Pringle finally retired. She obviously greeted my do-it-yourself plans with mixed feelings.

'It's a relief not to have our Minnie messing about with things,' she announced. 'Or anyone else, for that matter. I likes to know where to lay my hands on a piece of soap or a new dish-cloth, and where to hide the matches out of Bob Willet's way. I don't say he thieves. I'm not one to speak ill of anybody, but he sort of *borrers* them to light that filthy pipe of his, and pockets 'em absentminded. It's better there's no stranger trying to run the place.'

'I'm glad you like the idea,' I said. I was soon put straight.

'I *don't* like the idea!' boomed Mrs Pringle fortissimo. She spoke with such vehemence that I trembled for the safety of her operation scar.

'But what can I do?' she continued. 'Helpless, that's what I am, and I must just stand aside and watch them stoves rust, and the floor turn black, and the windows fur over with dust, while you and Bob Willet and the children turns a blind eye to it all.'

I said, humbly, that we would do our best, and that Mrs Willet had offered to oversee the washing-up at midday.

Mrs Pringle looked slightly mollified.

'Yes, well, that's something, I suppose. A drop in the ocean really, but at least Alice Willet knows what's what, and rinses out the tea clorths proper. Tell her I always hangs 'em on that little line by the elder bush to give 'em a bit of a blow, and then they finishes off draped over the copper.'

I promised to do so, and made a hasty departure.

'And tell Bob Willet not to lay a finger on them stoves,' she called after me. 'There's no need to light them for weeks yet.'

I let her have the last word.

Certainly, there was no need for the stoves on the first day of term. As so often happens, it dawned soft and warm, the morning·sky as pearly as a pigeon's wing, and the children appeared in their summer clothes.

They all seemed to be in excellent spirits as I passed through the throng from my house to the school, and as far as I could see, attendance would not be appreciably lower, despite the measles epidemic.

A few were disporting themselves on the pile of coke, as usual, and came down reluctantly when so ordered. Unseasonably, a number of the girls were skipping together in the remains of someone's clothes line.

They were chanting:

'*Salt, mustard, vinegar*',

And then, with an excited squeal: '*Pepper!*'

At which, the line twirled frenziedly, and some of the skippers were vanquished.

Three mothers waited with new children by the door, and I ushered them all in to enter the children for school.

Two I knew well, for both had sisters at the school, but the third was a stranger, a well-dressed dark-eyed boy of about nine.

'We're living at the cottage opposite Miss Waters,' his mother told me. 'My husband is at the atomic energy station.'

I remembered Mrs Johnson, who had lived there before, and prayed that the present tenant would not be such a confounded nuisance. She certainly seemed a pleasant person, and it looked as though Derek would be an intelligent addition to my class.

'Show Derek where to put his things, and look after him,' I said to Ernest, who was hovering near the door, anxious not to miss anything.

His mother made her farewells to the child briskly, smiled at us all and departed – truly an exemplary mother, I thought, and the boy went willingly enough with Ernest.

The other two would be entering the infants' class, and their mothers were rather more explicit in their farewells.

'Now, don't forget to eat up all your dinner, and ask the teacher if you wants the lavatory, and play with Susie at play time, and keep off of that coke, and use your hanky for lord's sake, child, and I'll see you at home time.'

Thus adjured, the children were taken into the infants' room, and I went out to call in the rest of my flock.

By age-old custom, the children are allowed to choose the hymn on the first morning of term. Weaning Patrick from

157

'Now the day is over', at nine in the morning, and Linda Moffat from 'We plough the fields and scatter', as being a trifle premature, we settled for 'Eternal Father, strong to save', for although we are about as far inland at Fairacre, as one can get in this island, we have a keen admiration for all sea-farers, and in any case, this majestic hymn is one of our favourites.

The new child, Derek, was standing near the piano and sang well, having a pure treble which might perhaps earn him a place at a choir school one day, I thought.

After prayers, we settled to the business of the day. Only five children were absent from my class, three with measles, one with ear-ache, and Eileen Burton for a variety of reasons supplied by her vociferous class-mates.

'Gone up her gran's,' said Patrick.

'No, she never then,' protested John. 'She's gone to Caxley with her mum about something on her foot.'

'A shoe perhaps,' commented some wag, reducing the class to giggles and much explaining of the joke to those who had been too busy chattering themselves to hear.

When order was restored, a more seemly set of reasons was offered for her absence. Someone said she was shopping, John stuck to the foot story with growing vehemence, someone else was equally positive that her mum was bad, while Joseph Coggs' contribution was that she was all right last night because she'd gone scrumping apples with him up Mr Roberts' orchard.

At this innocent disclosure, silence fell. I took advantage of it to point out, yet again, the evils of stealing, and, finally, requested Ernest and Patrick to give out the school books in preparation for a term of solid work.

Temporarily chastened, they settled down to some arithmetic in their rough books, with only minor interruptions such as:

'I've busted the nib off of my pencil.'

'Patrick never give me no book,' and other ungrammatical complaints which I, and thousands of other teachers, deal with automatically, with no disturbance to the main train of thought.

Before half an hour had gone by, however, the infants' teacher appeared at the partition door, holding one of the newcomers by the hand.

The little girl's face was pink with weeping. Tears coursed downward, and it was quite clear that the hanky, thoughtfully pinned by her mother to her frock, had not been used recently.

'Don't worry,' I said. 'Let her stay here with Margaret.'

Margaret, motherly in her solicitude, did some much-needed mopping, some kissing and scolding, and took her to sit beside her in the desk. The tears stopped as if by magic.

'Perhaps she would like a sweet,' I said, nodding towards the cupboard where a large tin of boiled sweets is kept for just such emergencies.

Margaret went to get it. There was an expectant hush in the classroom as the children watched the little one select a pear drop. Would I? Wouldn't I?

'You'd better take the tin round,' I said.

One needs something to help the first day along.

The golden day crawled by, and at the end of afternoon school I sauntered through the village to the Post Office to buy National Savings' stamps before Mr Lamb put up his shutters.

This was one of the jobs I should have done during the past week, but somehow the lovely holiday with Amy had unsettled me, and getting back to the usual routine had been extremely difficult.

I found my mind roving back to that delectable island, thinking of the white goats tossing their heads up and down as they nibbled carob branches, of the bearded priests, dignified in their black Greek Orthodox robes, of the smiling peasant we had met up in the hills, carrying a curly white lamb under each arm and the old woman sitting on her doorstep to catch the last of the light, intent upon her handspinning.

That dazzling light, which encompassed all out there, was unforgettable. It served, too, to make me more aware of the subtleties of gentler colour now that I was at home.

As I walked to the Post Office I saw anew how the terra cotta of the old earthenware flower pot in a cottage garden matched the colour of the robin's breast nearby. The faded green paint of Margaret Waters' door was echoed in the soft green of her cabbages. The sweet chestnut tree near the Post Office was thick with fruit, as softly-bristled as young hedge-hogs, and matching the lime-green tobacco flowers which are Mr Lamb's great pride.

Mrs Coggs was busy filling in a form, assisted by the postmaster. She wrote painfully and slowly, far too engrossed in the job to notice me, and I waited while Mr Lamb did his instructing.

'Now just your name, Mrs Coggs. Here, on this line.'

The pen squeaked, and I thought how patient he was, bending so kindly over his pupil. He moved, and a shaft of sunlight fell across Mrs Coggs' arms. I was disturbed to see that they were badly bruised, and so was the hand that held the pen so shakily.

'And here?' she asked, looking up.

'No, no need for you to fill that in. I can do that for you. That's all now, Mrs Coggs. I'll see to it.'

She gave a sigh of relief, and turned. I saw that one eye was black.

'Lovely day, miss. Had a nice holiday?'

'Yes, thank you. Are you all well?'

'Baby's teething, but the rest of us is doin' nicely.'

She nodded and smiled, and went out to the baby who was gnawing its fists in the pram.

'Doing nicely,' echoed Mr Lamb, when she had pushed the pram out of earshot. He put Mrs Coggs' form tidily, with others, in a folder.

'Beats me why she stays with that brute,' he went on. 'Did you see her arms? And that black eye?'

I nodded.

'I bet she copped that lot last Saturday. Arthur had had a skinful down at "The Beetle and Wedge", I heard. That chap drinks three parts of his wage packet – when he earns any, that is – and she's hard put to it to get the rent out of him.'

'I thought things seemed better now they were in a council house.'

Mr Lamb snorted, and began to open the folder holding savings' stamps without even asking my needs.

'Better? You'll never alter Arthur Coggs even if you was to put him in Buckingham Palace! Usual, I suppose?' he said, looking up.

'Yes, please.'

'Pity she never left him before all those children came. Now she's shackled, and he knows it. Gets her in the family way every two years or so, and there she is tied with another baby and another mouth to feed, poor devil.'

'I wonder how we can help,' I said, thinking aloud. 'It might be an idea to have a word with the district nurse.'

'If you're thinking she can help with the pill and that,' said Mr Lamb, 'you'll have to think again. If Arthur got wind of anything like that, he'd knock the living daylights out of the poor woman.

He folded the stamps and I put them in my bag. To my surprise, he looked rather embarrassed as he scrabbled in the drawer for my change.

'Shouldn't be talking of such things to a single lady like you, I suppose.'

I said that I had been conversant with the facts of life for some time now.

'Yes, well, no doubt. But you can take it from me, miss,

you've a lot to be thankful for, being single. When I see poor souls like Mrs Coggs coming in here, I wonder women get married at all.'

'Mrs Lamb seems happy enough,' I observed. 'Not all husbands are like Arthur Coggs, you know.'

'That's true,' conceded Mr Lamb. 'But nevertheless, you count your blessings!'

I pondered on Mr Lamb's advice as I walked back to the school house through the sunshine. It reminded me again of Amy's plight, of Mrs Clark's at the hotel, and of all the complications which, it seemed, married life could bring. Somehow, in the last few months, the advantages and disadvantages of the single and the married states had been thrust before me with disconcerting sharpness.

After tea, still musing, I took a walk through the little copse at the foot of the downs. Honeysuckle was in flower in the hedges, and the wood itself was heavy with the rich smells of summer. Yes, I supposed that I should count my blessings, as Mr Lamb had said. I was free to come and go as I pleased. Free to wander in a summer wood, when scores of other villagers were standing over stoves cooking their husbands' meals, or were struggling with children unwilling to go to bed whilst the sun still shone.

And yet, and yet. . . . Was I missing something as vital as Amy insisted? I remembered the sad monk at Toplou, the garrulous schoolteacher, the victim of loneliness, on the flight home, and a dozen more single people who perhaps were slightly odd when one came to think about them. But any odder than the married ones?

I began to climb the path up the downs beside a wire fence.

A poor dead rook had been hung there, as a warning, I supposed, to others. I looked at the glossy corpse with pity as it hung upside down, its beautiful wings askew, like some wind-crippled umbrella. How quickly life passed, and how easily it was extinguished!

I looked up at the downs and decided I should turn back. Moods of melancholy are rare with me, and this one had quite worn me out. What, I wondered, besides the encounter with Mrs Coggs, had brought it on? Could I, at my advanced age, be love-lorn, regretting my lost youth, pining for a state I had never known? A bit late in the day for that sort of thinking, I told myself briskly, and not the true cause of my wistfulness anyway.

It appeared much more likely to be caused by the first day of term combined with an unusually nasty school dinner.

I returned home at a rattling pace, ate two poached eggs on toast, and was myself again.

16 Gerard and Vanessa

ONE afternoon, a week later, I stood at my window and watched large hailstones bouncing on the lawn like mothballs. With any luck, the children should have got home before this sudden summer storm had broken, and any loiterers had only themselves to blame.

I was carrying out my tea tray to the kitchen when the telephone rang. It was Amy.

'Are you free this evening?'

'Yes. Anything I can do?'

'Yes, please. Come over to dinner. Gerard and Vanessa are here, just arrived. He's on his way to town, and has a lunch appointment tomorrow. I've persuaded him to stay the night. Do say you'll come.'

I said I should love to and would be with them at seven-thirty, if that suited her.

'Knowing you,' said Amy, 'you will be on the doorstep at seven-ten, asking what's on the menu. I warn you, mighty little! It's the company you're coming for!'

She rang off, and I was left to wonder how many times Amy has upbraided me for punctuality. Personally, I cannot bear to wait about for visitors who have been asked for seven or seven-thirty, and who elect to come at eight-fifteen while the potatoes turn from brown to black, and I stand enduring a fit of the fantods.

It was good to be going out, and I put on a silk frock which Amy had not yet seen, and hoped it would please her eye. I had seen nothing of her since our return, although we had spoken briefly on the telephone once or twice. How things were going with naughty James, I had no idea.

The hailstorm was over by the time I set out – carefully not too early – but it was cold and blustery. I took the back way to Bent, enjoying the distant view of the downs with the grey clouds scudding along their tops.

Vanessa opened the door to me. She was looking very pretty in a long blue frock, and her favourite piece of jewellery without which I have never seen her. It consists of a hefty brown stone, quite unremarkable, threaded on a long silver chain which reaches to her waist. I have nicer looking pebbles in the gravel of my garden path, but obviously Vanessa sets great store by this ornament, and one can only suppose that she has sentimental reasons for wearing it.

'Lovely to see you again,' she said, kissing my cheek, much to my surprise. 'Come and see Gerard. He brought me down, as I've some leave due to me, and Aunt Amy said I could come here for a few days.'

Gerard was as pink and cheerful as ever.

'Doesn't he look well?' commented Amy, 'I'm so glad he's staying the night. He's meeting his publisher tomorrow. It sounds important, doesn't it?'

'It is to me,' said Gerard. 'They're suggesting that I attempt another book. We're meeting to see how the land lies.'

'But what about the Scottish poets?' I asked.

'Ticking over nicely. I should get them done within a month or so.'

We talked of this and that over our drinks, and I had to

give him the latest news of Fairacre, with particular reference to Mr Willet and our local poet, Aloysius Stone, now long-dead, but not forgotten, in the parish.

Over dinner Amy told him about Crete with many interruptions from me. The black silk scarf had been received by Vanessa with expressions of joy and, what's more, with an offer to pay for it which had taken Amy completely off-guard.

'Of course, I couldn't possibly allow it,' she said to me privately afterwards. 'But I was very much touched by the offer. I must say Eileen's brought her up very well.'

As always, Amy's scratch meal turned out to be far more sophisticated and enjoyable than one had been led to expect.

After avocado pears stuffed with shrimps, we had a beef casserole and then fruit salad. I sat enjoying the fruit and thinking idly how typical it was of Amy to be able to produce avocado pears, not to mention everything else, at an hour or so's notice.

'This sliced banana,' said Vanessa dreamily, 'lying on my plate, is wizened to the likeness of a cat's anus.'

'*Really!*' exclaimed Amy, putting down her spoon with a clatter.

'Oh, it's only a quotation,' explained Vanessa, becoming conscious of our startled gaze upon her. 'One of our waiters is a poet, and he wrote it.'

'Well, I don't think he should be quoted at table, if that's typical of his work,' said Amy severely.

'He's really terribly gifted. He's had a book of poems published. I meant to tell you, Gerard dear. You may be able to help him. He paid three hundred pounds, he told me, to have them printed.'

167

'More fool him,' said Gerard.

'But couldn't you put in a word for him tomorrow when you meet your publisher?'

'I have more respect for my publisher than to lumber him with that sort of twaddle. I should say your waiter friend wants definite discouragement.'

'He's a very good waiter.'

'Then let him stick to his last,' advised Gerard. 'A good waiter's more use in the world than a poor poet.'

Vanessa sighed.

'I asked Angus if he could help. His father runs a Scottish evening paper, but they don't print poetry, he said.'

'Angus has tact.'

'And Ian Murray too, but he was no help. In fact, he used a terrible Scotch word about my poor little poet. I didn't quite understand it, and he refused to explain.'

'Ian Murray has been properly brought up.'

'And as for Andrew Elphinstone-Kerr, he simply roared his head off!'

'Do all your friends have such very Scotch names?' enquired Amy.

Vanessa's blue eyes opened very wide.

'Well, they do *live* in Scotland, Aunt Amy, and were born and bred there, so it's hardly surprising, is it? Apart from being so horrid to my waiter,' she added, 'I love them all.'

'I'm glad to hear you've made so many friends,' said Amy. 'We were interested to hear you had met Hattie May. How is she?'

'Quite spry, really, considering she's so old.'

'So old?' we echoed in unison.

'What nonsense!' said Amy, 'she's only a year or two older than I am.'

'I'm sorry,' began Vanessa, 'I forgot that you used to see her.'

'We never missed one of her shows,' I said.

'They're reviving one,' said Gerard. 'In fact, Miss May is in town at the moment for the first night. There's to be a party afterwards.'

'And Gerard's been invited,' said Vanessa.

'Only because she heard that I would be in town,' explained Gerard. 'I knew her husband, years ago, and then we met in Scotland at Vanessa's hotel.'

'You'll have a super time,' Vanessa enthused. 'I hope your evening clothes are up to the occasion.'

'I shall do my best to appear respectable,' Gerard assured her.

'Come and have coffee,' said Amy, leading the way to the drawing room. 'Would you like a tot of rum with it, Gerard?'

'Nothing I'd like more,' he replied.

Amy began clashing bottles in the cupboard.

'I'm so sorry, there doesn't appear to be any, and I was so looking forward to some myself. James usually keeps his eye on the drinks. Have whisky instead?'

'Let me run to the local,' said Gerard, 'and get you some rum. It would do me a world of good to get five minutes' exercise.'

After polite expostulations on Amy's side, he had his way, and set off accompanied by Vanessa.

The coffee percolator belched and burped companionably on the side table, as we waited.

'I wonder,' said Amy, sounding unusually wistful, 'whether anything will ever come of this affair. She seems so fond of Gerard.'

'She's also fond of half the eligible males in Scotland, as far as we can gather.'

'That's the pity of it. I really think that Gerard should realise that she won't hang about for ever. If he is really serious, I'm sure he should tell her so. Perhaps I could have a word with him. Tactfully, of course.'

'Amy,' I begged her. '*Say nothing*! They are both old enough to know what they are doing, and you will only cause everyone – including yourself – a great deal of embarrassment.'

'Perhaps you're right,' said Amy doubtfully. 'He's such a dear man, and it's time he was married. He'll start getting cranky if he waits much longer.'

'Gerard,' I said stiffly, 'is younger than I am.'

'That's what I mean,' replied Amy.

I was saved the necessity of answering by the arrival of Gerard, Vanessa and a large bottle of rum. And I was relieved to find that the rest of the evening passed without any reference to matrimony.

When the time came for me to go, Amy accompanied me to the car. A half-moon, low on the horizon and lying on its back, glowed as tawny as a ripe apricot.

'I haven't had a chance to tell you about James,' began Amy. She shivered. The night air was chilly.

'Get in the car,' I advised. 'We'll be more comfortable.'

'He came down last weekend, and we tried to have a straight talk. But oh, it's so sad! After all our years together we're becoming like strangers. I don't think I can bear it any longer. He's beginning to loathe me. I can see it in his face. Something will have to happen.'

'In what way?'

'I felt sure that I was right to give this matter time to fizzle out. Somehow I still think it will – but perhaps that's simply wishful thinking. I just don't know. All I can be sure of now, since we've been back from our holiday, is that he's getting more and more desperately unhappy.'

She fumbled for a handkerchief and blew her nose. After a moment or two, she went on.

'Now I ask myself, am I right in making three lives miserable? Has the time come to put my pride in my pocket and give in? Or am I right in thinking that one day he will give her up, and then need me? You can see how I torture myself. The position's getting more painful daily. What can I do?'

The question hung between us. A pinkish light from the rising moon warmed the front of Amy's pretty house. From the woods behind us, an owl cried.

'Amy,' I said slowly, 'I honestly don't know. I just can't think what sort of advice one could give in such a situation. I'm no help to you, and how desperately I wish I could be!'

Amy dabbed at her eyes.

'I wouldn't want my worst enemy to go through the misery I've had during these last few months. I feel torn this way and that. Whichever path I choose may be the wrong one.'

She sighed, put her damp cheek against mine, and then opened the door.

'I must go back. Thank you for coming, and for being such a prop in a tottering world. I'll give you a ring later on.'

I started the car and drove slowly down the drive. For the first time, the lonely figure I left standing in the doorway looked old and defeated, and I drove home struggling with tears of my own.

*　　　*　　　*

Soon after this evening with Amy, I had to keep an appointment at Caxley Hospital. This was to check that the broken arm was in good trim, and as I could do practically everything with it I had no doubt that I should be paying my last visit there.

The time of the appointment was three-thirty on a Wednesday afternoon, which meant that I should have to leave school at three, no doubt arriving at the hospital waiting room to find a score of other unfortunates called imperiously for exactly the same time.

I explained to my class that they must work on their own for the last half-hour or so, that Miss Edwards would leave the partition door ajar between the two rooms, and would keep an eye on them.

They knew, of course, that I was off to hospital, and were suitably impressed, not to say ghoulish, about it.

'Will they have to break it again? They did my dad's – to reset it.'

'I sincerely hope not.'

'Will you be put to bed?'

'Good heavens, no.'

'Will you come to school tomorrow?'

'Of course. Now stop fussing and get on with your work.'

Reluctantly, they took up their pens again.

After play, the new child, Derek, distributed boxes of crayons and enormous sheets of paper.

'You can draw a picture,' I told them, 'about any episode in history that you like.' This, I felt, should provide plenty of scope for the boys, who would settle, no doubt, for scenes of warfare involving a great many human figures in various attitudes both upright and prone, and for the girls who would probably decide to illustrate such events as Queen Victoria hearing of her accession, or Henry the Eighth meeting one of his wives, and needing a good deal of detailed work on the costumes. Such subjects should keep them busily scribbling until the end of school.

But for good measure, I wrote my old friend CONSTANTI-NOPLE on the blackboard, and supplied an extra piece of paper, to be folded long-wise into four, for lists of words made from that trusted standby.

'And you are to work quietly,' I said, 'and be a good example to the infants.'

They assumed unnatural expressions of virtue and trust-worthiness, I bade farewell to the infants' teacher, and set off.

I arrived at the hospital in good time, and followed a fellow-patient to the waiting room. She was on two sticks, and attended by an anxious daughter. The path led by a devious route to the back portions of the building and was composed of so much broken asphalt, pot-holes, manhole covers and the like, that it was a wonder that anyone arrived at the waiting room without injury, I reflected, as I picked my way cautious-ly between the laurel bushes.

There were quite a few of us hurt and maimed distributed on the benches. Legs in plaster casts, arms supported at shoulder level, people with slings, people with bandages – it might well have been the aftermath of just such a battle scene as those being created at Fairacre School.

I sat in the middle of an empty bench, but was joined within two minutes by a mountainous woman with a bandaged leg who told me, in hideous detail, what was concealed beneath her wrappings. I learnt more about the vascular system of the human frame, in that unfortunate ten-minute encounter, than I wished to know, and it was a relief to hear my name called and to be ushered into the doctor's presence.

He seemed a morose young man, and he had my sympathy.

'And how is it going, Mrs Potter?' he asked. I said I was Miss Read, and he put down the photographs he was studying rather hastily, and fished out another envelope.

'Of course, Mrs Read.'

'I'm single,' I said. He appeared not to hear, and I remained Mrs Read throughout the interview.

He felt my elbow, and then directed me to put my arm into various positions. The results seemed to depress him.

'Yes. Well, you shouldn't be able to do that with your injury. It pains you, I expect, Mrs Read?'

'Not at all.'

He looked disbelieving, and took a firm grip on the upper arm with one hand and the lower with the other hand, and tried a wrenching movement.

I yelped. An expression of satisfaction spread over his dour countenance.

'Still some need for improvement,' he said smugly. 'Keep on with the exercises. No need to come again, Mrs Read.'

He shook my hand warmly. No doubt about it, I had made his day.

The mountainous woman was on her way in as I came out.

'Coming again?' she asked.

'No!' I cried triumphantly, and made my escape into the sunshine.

17 A Visit From Miss Clare

ONE blue and white October day, I went to Beech Green to fetch Miss Clare who was going to pay a visit to Fairacre School where she had taught the infants for so many years.

Miss Clare, now a very old lady, lived alone in a thatched cottage which had been her home since early childhood. She was always invited to school functions, and was greeted with much affection by many of the Fairacre parents who owed their own early education to her efforts.

But today's visit was somewhat different. I had long been aware of the avid interest, shown by the older children, in the accounts of life in their village as remembered by their grandparents and other folk of that generation. Mr Willet's memories frequently enliven our schoolroom, and naturally, these firsthand accounts of local history have far more impact on the children than something read in a book.

Miss Clare, who had been a pupil as well as a teacher at our school, was willing to come and talk to the children, and as soon as school dinner was cleared away, I drove to Beech Green to collect her.

As always, she looked immaculate. She wore a navy-blue suit, and a very pale blue jumper under it. I admired the colour which matched her eyes.

'Dear Emily knitted it a few months before she died,' she

said calmly, speaking of her life-long friend who had shared her cottage for the last few years of her life. 'I keep it for best. I should like it to last.'

She was carrying a basket, covered with a white cloth, which she insisted on holding herself. She nursed it carefully throughout the journey and I wondered what it contained.

She was as long-sighted as ever, and on our drive back she pointed out a hovering sparrowhawk, which I confess I should have missed completely, and a weasel which emerged from the grass verge for an instant before turning tail and scurrying back to cover. Her mind was as keen as her eyesight, and she regaled me with snippets of Beech Green gossip, and with future plans for her garden, and a description of some new curtains she was sewing for her bedroom, until I began to feel lazier and more inefficient than ever.

She was greeted with enthusiasm by my class when we entered. Genuine affection, I knew, inspired nine-tenths of their exuberance, but I was aware that the fact that they would not need to exert themselves in work of their own that afternoon, partly contributed to their jubilation.

We set the most comfortable chair close to the front row, and the children at the back of the classroom came forward to squeeze companionably three in a desk, so that every word of Miss Clare's should be heard.

I sat at my desk and watched their intent faces. Certainly, Miss Clare had lost none of her old magic in holding children's interest.

The contents of the basket emerged one by one. The first object to be held up was a small china mug with a picture of Queen Victoria on the side.

'We all had one of these given to us,' she told the children,

'when the good Queen had reigned for sixty years. It was called her Diamond Jubilee, and you can see it written here.'

'Were you in this school then?' asked Linda Moffat.

'No, my dear, I was at Beech Green School then.' She went on to describe the junketings of that far-distant day when she was a young child, joining with her sister Ada, in the sports arranged in a nearby field.

She told them how she came to Fairacre School a year or two later, carefully omitting the reason, which I knew, for the move. A weak headmaster, with views too advanced for his time, had caused so much concern among the parents that several of them had transferred their children to other local

178

schools, despite the long walks, in every kind of weather, which this involved.

Miss Clare described those daily walks. It was almost three miles from her cottage to the school, and she told the wondering class where she found a robin's nest one spring, and where a tiny river once overflowed one February, and she and Emily Davis, her friend, took off their boots and stockings to paddle through the flood to get to school.

She showed them more treasures from her basket. A starched white pinafore, 'kept for Sundays', intrigued the girls who admired the insertion down the front as it was passed round the class for them to examine.

Her first copybook from Beech Green School with rows and rows of pot-hooks and hangers on the first few pages, and maxims of a strong moral flavour on the rest, was a source of wonder, but the object which gave them most excitement was the photograph of the whole of Fairacre School taken outside in our playground with Mr Wardle, the then headmaster, his wife, the infants' teacher Miss Taylor, and Dolly herself and Emily Davis as pupil teachers, standing meekly at one side of the rows of children. The clothes of the latter caused hilarity and a certain amount of sympathy.

'What's he doin' with that great ol' thing round his neck?' asked Patrick, gazing with bewilderment at one boy sporting an Eton collar. And the fact that nearly all the children wore lace-up boots, despite the brilliant sunshine which had caused most of them to screw up their eyes against the dazzle, puzzled my class considerably.

She described the village as she remembered it so long ago, telling of houses and barns now vanished, of splendid trees, which had towered over the roofs, felled years before, of a disused chapel, now turned into a house, and a host of other changes in their environment. The questions came thick and fast, and she answered all with care and composure.

The last thing to be brought from the basket, for the children's delectation, was a fine Bible.

'I was lucky enough to win the Bishop's Bible,' she told them. 'I sat just there, where Ernest is sitting, and it rained so hard that we could hardly hear the questions, I remember.'

The Bishop's Bible is still presented annually to the child who seems best grounded in religious knowledge, so that many a child in the class had just such a Bible at home, presented to a parent or relative years before. It seemed to bring home to them the continuity of tradition in this old school, and the bond between the Victorian child and those of the present day was forged even more firmly in Miss Clare's last few minutes with the class.

Patrick, primed and rehearsed beforehand, thanked her beautifully, and the children were sent to play.

I feared that she might be tired by her efforts, but she seemed stimulated, and insisted on calling on the infants after play where she spent the rest of the school afternoon.

'D'you reckon,' said Ernest, 'that you'll live as long as Miss Clare?'

I said I doubted it.

'Why not?' chorused the class.

'Children nowadays,' I told them, with as much solemnity as I could muster, 'are not as well-behaved as those Miss Clare taught. Teachers today get worn out before their time.'

They smiled indulgently at me, and at one another.

I would have my little joke!

*   *   *

Miss Clare came over to the school house for tea when school was over. One last object, not shown to the children, was produced. It was a pot of her own plum jam which made a most welcome addition to my larder.

The fire crackled merrily for I had slipped across during playtime to put a match to it. Outside, the shadows were already beginning to lengthen, and the chill of autumn became apparent as evening fell.

'It's a time of year I love,' said Miss Clare, stirring her tea. 'I love to see the barns full of straw bales, and to know the grain is safely stored, and to watch them ploughing Hundred Acre Field ready for another crop. I always feel when the harvest's home, that that's the true end of one year and the beginning of the next.'

'I must admit,' I agreed, 'that there's something very satisfying in pulling up all the tatty annuals and having a gorgeous bonfire in the garden. I like to think it's simply an appreciation of good husbandry, but I know that it's partly the thought of being relieved of gardening for a few months. And it's a positive pleasure to see the lawn mower go for its annual overhaul at the end of the summer. The older I get the less I enjoy pushing a mower. Mr Willet does it quite often, but he has so much to do in the village I don't rely on him.'

Miss Clare sighed.

'A man is *useful*! I suppose, if we're honest, we miss having husbands.'

'Like most things, there are points for and against husbands.' I told her about Mrs Coggs.

'I hope she's an exception, poor woman. It isn't only as a husband that Arthur Coggs fails. He's a complete failure at everything else. He won't work, he drinks, he lies and he sponges on the rest of us. But, after all, he's not typical of most men, and personally I very much regret that I did not marry.'

'You surprise me. I've always thought of you as one of the happiest, most serene people I know, with a perfectly full and satisfying life.'

Miss Clare smiled.

'I *am* happy. And, of course, one fills one's life whether single or married. I don't say that I sit and mope about being a spinster. I'm much too aware of my good fortune in having a home of my own, in a place I love, among a host of friends. But it's natural, I think, to wish to have someone of the next generation to carry on one's traditions and work. No, I think if I had been able to marry Arnold, I should truthfully have been happier still.'

She fingered the gold locket, which she always wears, containing the photograph of her fiancé so tragically killed in the First World War.

'After Arnold, there was nobody whom I could care for enough to marry. In any case, there was a dearth of young men after those terrible four years of war, and here in Fairacre and Beech Green, of course, men were few and far between anyway, and we hardly ever went further afield than Caxley, to meet others.'

This was true. When one came to think of it, those couples of Miss Clare's generation were probably born and brought up within a very few miles of each other. More probably still, they were related, which accounted for the few names in those old registers shared by a large number of children.

'No cars, no holidays abroad,' I said, thinking aloud. 'It certainly restricted one's choice.'

'Not only that. There were so few openings for girls and boys. I could either go into domestic service, or a shop, or nursing or teaching. Really there was nothing else open to a girl from a poor home. Nowadays, the young things go all over the world, or get a grant for further education somewhere miles from their own area, where they meet scores of other young people from all walks of life. No wonder they seem so sophisticated compared with ourselves at that age!'

'But are they happier?'

'When it comes to marriage, I have my doubts. In our day, we took our marriage vows pretty seriously and divorce was difficult and expensive. You knew you must make a go of the affair. Maybe there was a lot of unhappiness which was kept hidden, but on the whole I think the young people did better when they waited for each other and got to know themselves more thoroughly.'

Tibby arrived on the window sill, mouthing her complaints. I hurried to let her in. Her fur was fresh and cold, smelling of dry grass, bruised leaves and all outdoors.

'You would make a very good wife yourself,' said Miss Clare, watching me pour some milk into a saucer for my domestic tyrant.

'The chance would be a fine thing,' I replied. 'No, I haven't the pluck to risk it, even if I did have the chance. The single state suits me very well.'

'Tell me more about Crete,' said Miss Clare, and in that moment I knew that Amy's troubles were known to her and, no doubt, to most other people in the neighbourhood. Nothing had been said, and certainly not by me, but here it was again – that extraordinary awareness by country people of what is going on about them.

I launched enthusiastically into an account of all the wonders I had seen, and out came the photographs and maps and guide books.

It was past seven o'clock when I finally drove her home, and never once was Amy's name spoken between us.

Nevertheless, I knew Amy's affairs were now common knowledge, and I was not surprised.

Mrs Pringle's return to her duties I greeted with mingled relief and apprehension. We had done our best, in the last few weeks, to keep things clean and tidy, but I doubted if our standards would please Mrs Pringle.

I did not doubt for long.

''Ere,' said the lady, issuing from the back lobby where the washing up is done. 'What's become of my mop? Alice Willet thrown it out?'

I said I did not know.

'Hardly worn, that mop. A favourite of mine. Hope nothing's become of it.'

I thought of the character in *Cold Comfort Farm* who had the same affection for his little twig mop.

'Perhaps it's been put somewhere different,' I suggested weakly.

'*Everything*, as far as I can see,' boomed Mrs Pringle, 'has been put somewhere different. And the bar soap's almost gone, and them matches is standing for all to see and help themselves to.'

This was a side-swipe at Mr Willet, luckily not present, or battle would have been joined without hesitation.

'And where's the little slatted mat I stands on at the sink?' demanded the lady.

'I think it got broken.'

'Then the office should send out another. If I have to stand on damp concrete, in my state of health, I'll be back in Caxley Hospital before you can say "knife".'

I said that I would indent for another mat without delay.

Mrs Pringle prowled around my classroom, sniffing suspiciously.

'Funny smell this place has got. You been letting the mice in?'

'Is it likely?' I responded coldly. 'Do you imagine I spread a mouse banquet of cheese crumbs and bacon rinds and then open the door and invite them in?'

'There's no saying,' was Mrs Pringle's rejoinder. She ran a fat finger along the top of a door and surveyed the resulting grime.

'And not much dustin' done neither,' she commented.

'The children can't reach the tops of the doors.'

'There's others who can,' she answered.

As usual, I could see that I should lose this battle. Luckily, at this juncture, the new boy Derek appeared on the scene with a cut finger, and I was obliged to break off our exchanges and attend to him.

As I wrapped up his finger, I noticed his eyes were fixed on Mrs Pringle who still roamed the room, sniffing and making small noises of disapproval as she examined cupboard tops, window sills, and even the inside of the piano.

'Off you go,' I said, when I had completed my first aid. 'Try and keep it clean.'

Mrs Pringle made her way into the infants' room. No doubt she would find plenty there to gloat over, I thought.

Through the open window I became conscious of two voices. One belonged to Derek.

'Who's that lady in there?'

'Ma Pringle.'

'What does she do? Is she a teacher?'

'Nah! Old Ma Pringle? She's the one what keeps the school clean.'

'But I thought we did that?'

'You thought wrong then, mate. We done a bit while she was ill, but I bet Ma Pringle don't reckon we've kept it clean!'

Too true, I thought, too true!

18 Autumn Pleasures

SATURDAY mornings are busy times for school-teachers. It is then that they usually tackle the week's washing, any outstanding household jobs and, of course, the week-end shopping.

The latter can usually be done in Fairacre, but this Saturday in question I found that I needed such haberdashery items as elastic and pearl buttons. As there were one or two garments to be collected from the cleaners as well, I faced the fact that I must get out the car and make a sortie into Caxley.

While I was choosing a piece of rock salmon for Tibby and two fillets of plaice for myself, Amy smote me on the back.

As usual, she was looking as if she had come out of a bandbox, elegant in dark green with shoes to match. I became conscious of my shabby camel car coat, heavily marked down the right sleeve with black oil from the lock of the car door, and my scuffed car shoes.

'Nearly finished?' she asked.

'Just about. A pound of sprouts, and I'm done.'

'Let's have a spot of lunch together at "The Bull",' suggested Amy. 'They do some very good toasted sandwiches in the bar, and I'm famished.'

'So am I. An hour's shopping in Caxley finishes me. Partly, I think, it's the smug pleasure with which half the assistants tell you they haven't got what you want.'

'And that it's no good ordering it,' added Amy. 'I know. I've been suffering that way myself this morning.'

I bought my sprouts, and we entered 'The Bull'. A bright fire was welcoming and we sank gratefully into the leather armchairs to drink our sherry. We were the only people in the bar at that moment, for we were early. Within a short time, the place would be crowded.

'Vanessa's back at work,' said Amy.

'Did Gerard take her to Scotland?'

'Oh no, he's back in London in his little flat, putting the final touches to the book, I gather. A very personable young man picked her up. I never did catch his name. Could it have been Torquil?'

'Sounds likely. I take it he was a Scot?'

'They're *all* Scots at the moment, which makes me anxious about Gerard. He really should be a little more alert if he wants to capture Vanessa.'

'Perhaps he doesn't.'

Amy's mouth took on a determined line.

'I'm quite sure *she* is fond of him. She talks of him such a lot, and is always asking his advice. You know, she really *respects* Gerard. Such a good basis for a marriage where there is a difference in age.'

'Well, there's nothing you can do about it,' I pointed out. 'Have another sherry?'

I went to get our glasses refilled. Amy was looking thoughtful as I replaced them on the table by the sandwiches.

'James was down during the week,' she said. 'He looks worried to death. I don't know whether the girl is wavering and he is having to increase his efforts, or whether he senses that *I'm* wavering, but something's going to give before long.

And I've a horrible feeling it's going to be me. It's an impossible situation for us all. What's more, I keep getting tactful expressions of sympathy from people in the village, and I'm not sure that that isn't harder to bear than James's indiscretions.'

I remembered Miss Clare.

'You can't keep any secrets in a village,' I said. 'You know that anyway. Don't let that add to your worries.'

'But how do people find out? I've not said a word to a soul. Even Mrs Bennet, our daily, knows nothing.'

'You'd be surprised! A lot of it's guesswork, plus putting two and two together and making five. Bush telegraph is one of the strongest factors in village life, and works for good as well as ill. Look how people rallied when I broke my arm!'

'Which reminds me,' said Amy, looking at her watch. 'I must get back to pack up the laundry. Mrs Bennet hasn't been for the last two days. She's down with this wretched measles. Caught it from her grandchild.'

'There's a lot about. Three more cases last week in the infants' room.'

'There's talk of closing Bent School,' Amy told me. 'Actually, they rang up last week to see if I could do some supply work there, but I felt I just couldn't with James coming down, and so much hanging over me. They're two staff short, and no end of children away.'

'Have you had it?'

'What, measles? Yes, luckily, at the age of six or seven, and all I can remember is a bowl of oranges permanently by the bedside, and the counterpane covered with copies of *Rainbow* and *Tiger Tim's Annual*.'

We collected our shopping and made for the door, much fortified by 'The Bull's' hospitality.

'I wonder if I've got the stamina to go looking for a new winter coat,' I mused aloud.

Amy eyed my dirty sleeve.

'You certainly look as though you need one,' she commented.

'The thing is, should it be navy blue or brown? In a weak moment last year I bought a navy blue skirt and shoes, and I ought to make up my mind if I'm to continue with navy blue, which means a new handbag as well, or play safe with something brown which will go with everything else.'

Amy shook her head sadly.

'Well, I can't spare the time to come with you, I'm afraid. What problems you set yourself! And you know why?'

I shook my head in turn.

'*No method!*' said Amy severely, waving goodbye.

She's right, I thought, watching her trim figure vanishing down the street.

I decided that I could not face such a problem at the moment, collected my car and drove thankfully along the road to Fairacre.

The conker season was now in full swing. Rows of shiny beauties, carefully threaded on strings, lined the ancient desk at the side of the room, and as soon as playtime came, they were snatched up and their owners rushed outside to do battle.

There were one or two casualties understandably. Small boys, swinging heavy strings of conkers, and especially when faced with defeat, are apt to let fly at an opponent. One or two bruises needed treatment, usually to the accompaniment of heated comment.

'He done it a-purpose, miss.'

'No, I never then.'

'I saw him, miss. Oppin mad, he was, miss.'

'Never! I saw him too, miss. They was jus' playin' quiet-like. It were an accident.'

'Cor! Look who's talking! What about yesterday, eh? You was takin' swipes at all us lot, with your mingy conkers.'

'Whose mingy conkers? They beat the daylights out of yourn anyway!'

Luckily, the conker season is a relatively short one, and the blood cools as the weather does.

Out in the fields the tractors were ploughing and drilling. We could hear the rooks, dozens of them, cawing as they followed the plough, flapping down to grab the insects turned up in the rich chocolate-brown furrows.

The hedges were thinning fast, and a carpet of rustling leaves covered the school lane. Scarlet rose hips and crimson hawthorn berries splashed the hedgerows with bright colour, and garlands of bryony, studded with berries of coral, jade and gold, wreathed the hedges like jewelled necklaces.

The children brought hazel nuts and walnuts to school, cracking them with their teeth, and as bright-eyed and intent as squirrels as they examined their treasures. Their fingers were stained brown with the green husks from the walnuts, and purple with the juice from late blackberries. Plums and apples from cottage gardens joined the biscuits on the side table ready for playtime refreshment. Autumn is the time of plenty, of stocking up for the lean days ahead, and Fairacre children take full advantage of nature's bounty.

So do the adults. We were all busy making plum jam and apple jelly, and keeping a sharp eye on the wild crab apples which would not be ready until later. There are several of these trees among the copses and hedges of Fairacre, and most years there is plenty of fruit for everyone. One year, however, soon after I arrived in Fairacre, there was a particularly poor crop of these lovely little apples. A newcomer to the village, one of the 'atomic wives', living in the cottage now inhabited by young Derek and his parents, was rash enough to pick the lot, much to the fury of the other good wives of Fairacre. I remember, in my innocence, attempting to be placatory, suggesting that ignorance, rather than greed, had prompted her wholesale appropriation.

'We'll learn her!' had been the vengeful cry. And they did. Perhaps it was as well that her husband was posted elsewhere after this unfortunate incident. I can't think that she really enjoyed her crab apple jelly.

There is a very neighbourly feeling about picking these wild fruits, and very few would strip a hedge of nuts or blackberries. Leaving some for the next comer is usual. It is as though the generosity of nature communicates itself to those blessed by it, and many a time I have heard the children, and their parents, recommending this hedge or that tree as the best place to try harvesting.

One of the group of elms at the corner of the playground was considered unsafe and had to come down. The children were allowed to watch the operation at a respectful distance. The two men had the small branches off, the trunk sawn through and the giant toppled, all within the hour.

It fell with a dreadful cracking sound, and thumped into Mr Roberts' field beyond. The children raised a great shout of triumph, but one of the infants grew tearful and said:

'I don't like it falling down.'

'Neither do I,' I said. We seemed to be the only two who

felt saddened at the sight. Everyone else rejoiced, but I cannot see a tree felled, particularly a majestic one such as this was, without a shock of horror at the swift killing of something which has taken a hundred years or more to grow, and has given shelter and beauty to the other lives about it.

However, I was not too shattered to be grateful for some of its logs which Mr Willet procured for me. I helped him to stack them in my wood shed one afternoon after school.

The sky was that particularly intense blue which occasionally occurs in October. Across the fields, in the clear air, the trees glowed in their russet colours. It was invigorating handling the rough-barked wood, knowing that the winter's fires would be made splendid with its burning.

But it was cold too. Mr Willet, stacking the final few, blew out his moustache.

'Have a frost tonight, you'll see. Got your dahlias up?'

I had not. Mr Willet evinced no surprise.

'Shall I do 'em for you now?' he offered.

'No need. I've kept you long enough. It's time you were home.'

'That's all right. Alice has gone gadding into Caxley to a temperance meeting.'

Gadding seemed hardly the word to use under the circumstances, I felt.

'Come and have a cup of tea with me then,' I said. We stood back to admire the stack of logs before making for the kitchen.

'That baby of Mrs Coggs has got the measles, they say,' said Mr Willet, stirring his tea. 'Them others away from school?'

'Not today. I'd better look into it. Two more infants are down with it, but we're not as badly off as Bent.'

I told him what Amy had said about the possibility of the school there having to close.

'And how is your friend?' enquired Mr Willet. 'I did hear,' he added delicately, 'that she was in a bit of trouble.'

Here we were again, I thought. I had no desire to snub dear old Mr Willet, but equally I had no wish to betray Amy's confidences.

'Aren't we all in a bit of trouble, one way or the other?' I parried.

'That's true,' agreed Mr Willet. 'But you single ones don't have the same trouble as us married folk. Only got yourself to consider, you see. Any mistakes you make don't rebound on the other like. Take them dahlias.'

'What about them?'

I was relieved that we seemed to have skated away from the thin ice of Amy's affairs.

'Well, if my Alice'd forgot them dahlias, I should have cut up a bit rough, seeing what they cost. But you, not having no husband, gets off scot free.'

'Not entirely. I shall have to pay for any new ones.'

'Yes, but that's your affair. There ain't no *upsets*, if you see what I mean. No bad feelings. You can afford to be slap-dash and casual-like. Who's to worry?'

I laughed.

'You sound like Mrs Pringle! Am I really slap-dash and casual, Mr Willet?'

'Lor, bless you,' said Mr Willet, rising to go, 'you're the most happy-go-lucky flibbertigibbet I've ever met in all me born days! Many thanks for the tea, Miss Read. See you bright and early!'

And off he went, chuckling behind his stained moustache, leaving me dumb-founded – and with all the washing-up.

I had time to savour Mr Willet's opinion of me as I sat knitting by the fire that evening. I was amused by his matter-of-fact acceptance of my shortcomings. His remarks about the drawbacks of matrimony I also knew to be true. Any unsettled feelings I had suffered during the holidays, had quite vanished, and I realised that I was back in my usual mood of thinking myself lucky to be single.

For some unknown reason I had a sudden craving for a pancake for my supper. I had not cooked one for years, and thoroughly enjoyed beating the batter, and cutting a lemon ready for my feast. I even tossed the pancake successfully, which added to my pleasure.

If I were having to provide for a husband, I thought, tucking into my creation, a pancake would hardly be the fare to offer as a complete meal. No doubt there would be 'upsets', as Mr Willet put it. Yes, there was certainly something to be said for the simple single life. I was well content.

The fire burnt brightly. Tibby purred on the rug. At ten o'clock I stepped outside the front door before locking up. There was a touch of frost in the air, as Mr Willet had forecast, and the stars glittered above the elm trees. Somewhere in the village a dog yelped, and near at hand there was a rustling among the dry leaves as some small nocturnal animal set out upon its foraging.

With my lungs full of clear cold air I went indoors and made all fast. I was in my petticoat when the telephone rang.

It was Amy. She sounded incoherent, and quite unlike her usual composed self.

'James has had an accident. I'm not sure where. In the car, I mean, and the girl, Jane, with him, I'm just off.'

'Where is he?'

'Somewhere near Salisbury, in a hospital. I've got the address scribbled down.'

'Shall I come with you?'

'No, no, my dear. I only rang because I felt someone should know where I was. Mrs Bennet's not on the phone, and any-way, as you know, she's ill. I must go.'

'Tell me,' I said, wondering how best to put it, 'is he much damaged?'

'I don't know. They told me nothing really. The hospital

people found his address on him and simply rang me to say he was there. He's unconscious – they did say that.'

I felt suddenly very cold. Was this the dreadful way that Amy's affairs were to be settled?

'Amy,' I urged, 'do let me come with you, please.'

I could hear her crying at the other end. It was unendurable.

'No. You're sweet, but I must go alone. I'll be careful, I promise. And I'll ring you first thing tomorrow morning when I know more.'

'I understand,' I said. 'Good luck, my love, and call on me if there's anything I can do to help.'

We hung up. Mechanically, I got ready for the night and climbed into bed, but there was no hope of sleeping.

I think I heard every hour strike from the church tower, as I lay there imagining Amy on her long sad journey westward, pressing on through the darkness with a chill at her heart more cruel than the frosts around her.

What awaited Amy at the end of that dark road?

19 James Comes Home

AFTER my disturbed night I was late in waking. Fortunately, it was Saturday, and my time was my own. I went shakily about the household chores, alert for the telephone bell and a message from Amy.

Outside, a wind had sprung up, rattling the rose against the window and ruffling the feathers of the robin on the bird table. Frost still whitened the grass, but great grey clouds, scudding from the west, promised rain before long with milder weather on the way.

The hands of the clock crept from nine to ten, from ten to eleven, and still nothing happened. My imagination ran riot. Was James dying? Or dead, perhaps, and Amy too distraught to think of such things as telephone calls? And what about the girl? Was she equally seriously injured? And what result would this accident have upon all three people involved?

I made my mid-morning coffee and drank more than half before realising that the milk was still waiting in the saucepan. A shopping list progressed by fits and starts, as I made one entry and then gazed unseeingly through the window.

Suddenly, the bell rang, and I was about to lift the receiver when I realised that it was the back door bell.

Mrs Pringle stood on the doorstep holding a fine cabbage.

'Thought you could do with it,' she said. 'I was taking the

school tea towels over the kitchen so thought I'd kill two birds with one stone.'

I thanked her and asked if she would like some coffee.

'Well, now,' she said graciously, 'I don't mind if I do.'

I very nearly retorted, as an ex-landlady of mine used to do when encountering this phrase:

'And I don't mind if you *don't*!' but I bit it back.

Mrs Pringle seated herself at the kitchen table, loosening her coat and rolling her hand-knitted gloves into a tidy ball.

I switched on the stove to heat the milk again. As one might expect, it was at this inconvenient moment that the telephone bell rang.

'Make the coffee when it's hot,' I cried to Mrs Pringle, and rushed into the hall.

It was Amy.

She sounded less distraught than the night before, but dog-tired.

'Sorry to be so late in ringing, but I thought I'd wait until the doctor had seen James, so that I had more news to tell you.'

'And what is it?'

'He's round this morning, but still in a good deal of pain. The collar bone is broken and a couple of ribs cracked, and he's complaining of internal pains. Still, he's all right, the doctor says, and can be patched up.'

'What about his head? Did he have concussion?'

I was suddenly conscious of Mrs Pringle's presence and, without doubt, her avid interest in the side of the conversation she could hear. Too pointed to close the kitchen door, I decided, and anyway too late.

'Yes. He was knocked out, and has a splitting head this morning, but, thank God, he'll survive.'

'Now, my dear, would you do something for me?'

'Of course. Say the word.'

'Could you pop over to Bent and take some steak out of the slow oven? Like an ass, I forgot it in the hurry last night. It's been stewing there for about fourteen hours now, so will probably be burnt to a frazzle.'

'What shall I do with it?'

'Let Tibby have it, if it's any use. Otherwise, chuck it out. And would you sort out the perishables in the fridge? And cancel the milk and bread? I'm sorry to bother you with all this, but I've decided to stay nearby. There's a comfortable hotel and James won't be able to be moved for a bit. Mrs Bennet isn't on the phone, and I don't like to worry her anyway while she's ill.'

I said I would go over immediately, scribbled down her forwarding address, and was about to put down the receiver when, luckily, Amy remembered to tell me where the spare key was.

'I've moved it from under the watering-can,' explained Amy, 'and now you'll find it inside one of those old-fashioned earthenware honey pots, labelled CARPET TACKS, on the top shelf at the left-hand side of the garden shed.'

I sent my love and sympathy to James.

'I'll ring again tomorrow,' promised Amy, and then the line went dead.

Mrs Pringle looked up expectantly as I returned, but I was not to be drawn.

'Have a biscuit, Mrs Pringle,' I said proffering the tin.

She selected a Nice biscuit with care. It was obviously a poor substitute for a morsel of hot news, but it had to do.

*　　*　　*

Half an hour later, I was on my way to Amy's, and it was only then that I remembered that nothing had been said about James's companion – Jane, wasn't it? What, I wondered, had happened to her?

The wind buffeted the car as I drove southward. The sheep were huddled together against the hedges, finding what shelter they could. Pedestrians were bent double against the onslaught, clutching hats and head-scarves, coat-tails flapping. Cyclists tacked dangerously to and fro across the road, dogs, exhilarated by the wind, bounded from verges, and children, screaming with excitement, tore after them.

The leaves of autumn, torn from the trees, fluttered down like showers of new pennies, sticking to the wind-screen, the bonnet, and plastering the road with their copper brightness. Amy's drive was littered with twigs and tiny cones from the fir tree which must have caught the full brunt of some particularly violent gust.

I found the key in the honey pot, and went indoors. A rich aroma of stewed beef greeted me, and my first duty was to rescue the casserole. Amazingly, it still had some liquor in it, and the meat had fallen into deliciously tender chunks. I decided that I should share this largesse with Tibby that evening.

Amy's refrigerator was far better stocked than mine, and much more tidy. There was little to remove – some milk, a portion of apricot pie, four sardines on a saucer, just the usual flotsam and jetsam of daily catering.

There were a few letters which I re-addressed, and then I wrote notes to the baker and milkman, before going round the house to make sure that the windows were shut and that any radiators were left at a low heat.

All seemed to be in order. I checked switches, locked doors, and took a final walk around Amy's garden, before replacing the key. It was while I was on my tour of inspection, that I saw a man battling his way from the gate.

He look surprised to see me.

'Oh, good morning! My name's John Bennet. My wife works here and asked me to come and see everything's all right.'

I asked after her.

'Getting on, but it's knocked all the stuffing out of her. These children's complaints are no joke when you're getting on.'

'So I believe. Don't worry about the house. Mrs Garfield asked me to look in. She's been called away.'

'Yes, we knew she must have been. That's why I came up. My sister, who lives just down the road from us, saw her setting off last night – very late it was – and looking very worried. My sister was taking out the dog, and guessed something must be up.'

I had imagined that Mrs Bennet had been concerned for any possible gale damage, but now revised my views.

'Mr Garfield,' I explained, 'has had a car accident, but is getting on quite well, I gather, and should be home before long. Tell Mrs Bennet not to worry. I'll keep an eye on the place while she's laid up, and if she wants to get in touch tell her to phone me.'

We took a final turn round the windy garden together before parting. All seemed well.

I got back into the car and set off for home, marvelling, yet again, at the extraordinary efficiency of bush telegraph in rural areas.

The gales continued for the rest of the week, and the children were as mad as hatters in consequence.

Wind is worse than any other element, I find, for causing chaos in a classroom. Snow, of course, is dramatic, and needs to be inspected through the windows at two-minute intervals to see if it is 'laying'. But this is something which occurs relatively seldom in school hours.

Sunshine and rain are accepted equably, but a good blustery wind which bangs doors, rattles windows, blows papers to the floor, and the breath from young bodies, is a fine excuse for boisterous behaviour.

Up here, on the downs, the wind is a force to be reckoned with. Not long ago, an elm tree crashed across the roof of St Patrick's church, and caused so much damage that the village was hard put to it to raise the money for its repair. Friends from near and far rallied to Fairacre's support, and the challenge was met, but we all, (and Mr Willet, in particular, who strongly suspects any elm tree of irresponsible falling-about through sheer cussedness), watch our trees with some apprehension when the gales come in force.

The only casualty this time, as far as I knew, was a venerable damson tree in Ernest's garden. He brought the remaining fruit to school in a paper bag, and the small purple plums were shared out among his school fellows.

I watched this generous act with some trepidation. Damsons, even when plentifully sugared, are as tart a fruit as one could wish to meet. To see the children scrunching them raw made me shudder, but apart from one or two who complained that 'they give them cat-strings' or 'turned their teeth all funny', Ernest's largesse was much enjoyed.

My own share arrived in the form of a little pot of damson

cheese, made by Ernest's mother, and for this I was truly thankful.

Apart from fierce cross-draughts, and a continuous whistling one from the skylight above my desk, we were further be-devilled by smoke from the tortoise stove. Even Mrs Pringle, who can control our two monsters at a touch, confessed herself beaten, so that we worked with eyes sore with smoke and much coughing – most of it affected – and plenty of smuts floating in the air.

Amy rang twice during the few days after the accident. The car, she said, on the first occasion, was beyond repair and James had been lucky to escape so lightly.

'And Jane?' I dared to ask.

'Simply treated here for superficial cuts on her face and a sprained wrist. She'd gone home by the time I arrived, fetched by mother. At least she'd had the sense to be wearing her seat belt. It saved her from hitting her head on the windscreen which is what happened to James.'

'And how is he?'

'Still running a temperature, which the doctor thinks is rather peculiar, I gather. He's very restless, and in pain, poor thing. He was terribly worried about Jane, but they've put his mind at rest about that.'

'Any chance of bringing him home?'

'They don't seem in any hurry to get rid of him. He's been strapped up and the collar bone set, and so on. And I'm afraid his beauty has been spoiled, at least for a time, as a little slice was cut off the end of his nose by the glass of the windscreen.'

'Oh, poor James!'

'He doesn't care about the look of it, but curses most horribly whenever he needs to blow it.'

I sent my sympathy, assured Amy that all was well at Bent, and we rang off.

I had not mentioned it to my old friend, but this was the evening when I had undertaken to give a talk to Fairacre Women's Institute about our holiday in Crete.

Accordingly, soon after her telephone call, I dressed in my best and warmest garments and got ready for my ordeal. The Mawnes had promised to bring a projector and I had looked out my slides into some semblance of order. Amy had offered her own collection, but under the circumstances, I had to make do with my inferior efforts. Luckily, the brilliant Cretan light had guaranteed success with almost all the exposures.

The village hall was gratifyingly full and a beautiful flower arrangement graced the W.I. tablecloth. Listening to the minutes, from the front row, I studied its form. This was obviously the handiwork of one of 'the floral ladies', expert in arrangement of colour and form with no 'Oasis' visible at all, as is usual with us lesser mortals. The whole thing had been fixed, with artistic cunning, to a mossy piece of wood, and I was so busy trying to work out how it was done, that it came as a severe shock to hear my name called and to be obliged to take the floor.

I began by a brief description of our journey out, and of the attractions of the hotel. The projector, operated by Mr Mawne, worked splendidly for he had brought the correct plug for the village hall socket, a rare occurrence on these occasions, and we were all duly impressed at such efficiency and foresight.

The vivid colours of the Cretan landscape were even more impressive on a grey October evening. The animals evoked cries of admiration, although someone commented that the

R.S.P.C.A. would never have let a poor little donkey *that* small, hump a great load like that! I had to explain that, despite appearances, those four wispy legs beneath the piles of brushwood were really not suffering from hardship and that the load was light in weight.

Knossos, of course, brought forth the most enthusiastic response. The great red pillars and the beautiful flights of stairs made spectacular viewing, and the frescoes of dolphins and bulls were much admired. Even the topless ladies were accepted, except for one gasp of shock from Mrs Pringle in the front row.

I ended in good time, for I had seen Mrs Willet go quietly into the kitchen to attend to the boiling water in the urn, and knew that coffee break was scheduled.

My final word was of thanks to Mr Mawne, who had so nobly coped with the projector, and to whom I felt I owed an apology as I had been unable to photograph the Cretan hawk for him.

At this, Mr Mawne came forward and began a description of the elusive bird. I must say, his grasp of the subject was profound, and by the time he had described its appearance in detail, its habits, its mode of flight and its diet, a good many ladies were consulting their wrist watches while Mrs Willet hovered by the kitchen door, coffee pot in hand.

Meanwhile, I had sat down in the front row beside Mrs Pringle, the better to enjoy Mr Mawne's impromptu discourse. It is this off-the-cuff situation which gives village meetings their particular flavour. Who wants to stick to such a dreary thing as an agenda? As everyone knows, the *real* business takes place on the way home, or an hour after the meeting finished, in the local pub.

Henry Mawne was just about to begin on the breeding habits and nesting sites of the hawk, and had broken off to suggest that he would just slip down to his house to fetch a reference book on the subject, if the ladies were agreeable, when Mrs Partridge, as President, bravely rose and checked the flow with her usual charm and aplomb. What was more, she invited her old friend to speak at one of the monthly meetings next year about any of his favourite birds.

'I am sure that they will soon be our favourites as well,' she finished, with a disarming smile, and Henry resumed his seat, flushed with pleasure, while Mrs Willet hastened to bring in the coffee amidst general relief.

I was presented with the magnificent flower arrangement, so that, all in all, the evening was a resounding success.

Amy's second call came soon after I returned from school the next day.

'There's a bit of a panic here,' said Amy calmly. 'Don't laugh, but poor James has the *measles*!'

'Oh no! As though he hasn't enough to put up with.'

'Exactly. I suppose he picked it up when he was at home recently. Mrs Bennet was about in the house then. It might have been contact with her. But there, it could have been *anyone*! The point is, the hospital people seem dead anxious to get rid of him before he gives it to the rest of the ward, so they tell me he is fit enough to go home tomorrow.'

'I bet he's pleased.'

'He is. So am I. It's funny they didn't spot this rash earlier, but I think they put it down to a fairly common reaction to anti-biotics, and in any case, he hasn't got a great many spots.'

'Can I do anything this end?'

'Yes, please. Could you turn up the heating, and get some milk and bread for us? I'll shop the next day when he's settled in.'

I said I could do whatever was needed.

'He's still at the soup and egg-and-milk stage. A front tooth was knocked out, which gives him a piratical look, and his mouth hurts him quite a bit.'

'He sounds as though he's taken quite a pasting.'

'Well, evidently he was turning right, and a van was coming behind him pretty swiftly, and James caught the full force of the impact. Luckily, nothing too serious seems to have resulted apart from the collarbone and ribs. It's just that he looks rather odd with his sliced nose and gappy smile. And, of course, it is rather ignominious to have the measles in your fifties! In fact, rather a humiliating end altogether to what was going to be a glamorous few days in Devonshire.'

'Does he feel that?' I asked hesitantly.

'Yes, he certainly does,' said Amy. 'Wasn't it Molière who said: "One may have no objection to being wicked, but one hates to be ridiculous"? Well, that sums up James's feelings at the moment.'

The pips went for the second time, and I felt we should terminate our conversation.

'What time do you expect to be home?'

'During the late afternoon, I imagine. We'll have to see the doctor here, and I shall drive slowly. The poor old thing is pretty battered and bruised. He'll go straight to bed, of course.'

I said that I would put hot bottles in the beds, and we rang off.

An hour or so later, I drove over to Bent to do my little duties.

I took with me a few late roses to cheer the invalid's room, and half a dozen of Mrs Pringle's new-laid eggs.

On the way, I left a message at the dairy and collected a brown loaf. The house struck pleasantly warm when I entered, but I duly turned up the heating and set a fire ready in the sitting room for Amy to light on her return.

There was little else to do except to fill the hot-water bottles and to transfer the few letters from the floor to the hall table. I was home again by eight o'clock to join Tibby by my own fire.

Leg upraised, she washed herself industriously, spitting out little balls of goosegrass on to the hearthrug. As cat-slave, I transferred them meekly from the rug to the fire, my thoughts with Amy and James.

They were much in my mind throughout lessons the next day. Soon after five, Amy rang to thank me for my ministrations.

'What sort of journey?'

'Better than I thought. He stood it very well, and feels easier now that he's in his own bed. His temperature is almost back to normal. I shall get our own doctor to call in tomorrow, but I think he'll mend fast now.'

There was relief and happiness in Amy's voice which I had not heard for many months.

And I knew, as Amy certainly must know, that, in every sense of the expression, James had come home.

20 The Final Scene

THE autumn gales gave way to a spell of quiet grey weather, and we were all mightily relieved. The stoves behaved properly, the children almost as well, and their parents finished tidying their gardens and generally set about preparations for the winter ahead.

Mist veiled the downs from sight. It hung, swirling sluggishly, in the lanes, and everything outdoors was damp to touch. Flagged paths and steps glistened, little droplets hung on the hedges, and nothing stirred.

All sound was muffled. Mr Roberts' sheep, in the field across the playground, sounded as though they bleated from as far away as Beech Green. The dinner van purred to a halt as mellifluously as a Rolls. Even the children's voices, as they played up and down the coke pile, were pleasantly muffled.

The measles epidemic seemed to be on the wane. Children returned, a little peaky perhaps, and certainly with tiresome coughs which persisted long after they were pronounced cured, but seemingly ready for work and secretly glad, I suspected, to have something to occupy them.

James's measles, and his general injuries, kept him resting for some time after his return home. Amy rang me one evening when I was busy with the local paper.

'Getting on quite well,' she replied in answer to my enquiries. 'But I really rang about something quite different. Have you seen the paper today?'

'I'm holding it.'

'Good. Look at page fourteen.'

'Hang on while I turn it over.'

I spread the paper on the hall floor and turned the pages.

'What about it?' I asked.

'Well, look at the photograph!'

Amy sounded impatient. I looked obligingly at some twenty photographs of local houses. At least six pages of *The Caxley Chronicle* are devoted to housing advertisements.

'Which one?'

'What do you mean, which one? There is only one.'

'On page fourteen? It's one of the advertisement pages. There are about two dozen photographs.'

There was an ominous silence. When Amy spoke next it was in the quiet controlled voice of a teacher driven to desperation by some particularly obtuse pupil.

'Which paper are you looking at?'

'*The Caxley Chronicle*. You said 'The Paper'. On Thursday, naturally, 'The Paper' is the local one.'

'I didn't mean that thing!' Amy shouted, with exasperation. 'How parochially minded can you get? Look at *The Daily Telegraph*.'

'I shall have to fetch it,' I said huffily. 'I haven't had time to look at it yet.'

I found page fourteen in the right periodical, and called excitedly down the telephone.

'Yes! Good heavens! Gerard!'

'As you say, "Good heavens, Gerard!" What do you think of that?'

The photograph showed a pretty woman in a fur coat holding hands with Gerard, who was looking remarkably smug and had a wisp of hair standing up in the wind like a peewit's crest.

Underneath it said:

"Miss Hattie May, the well-known musical comedy actress, after her marriage to Mr Gerard Baker at Caxton Hall."

'It's staggering, isn't it?' I said. 'And they've even got the names right!'

'It's not the reporters I'm concerned with,' said Amy severely, 'it's poor Vanessa. What will she be feeling?'

'I don't imagine she'll be too upset,' I said. 'I never did think she was in love with him.'

This was plain speaking, but I was still smarting from Amy's high-handedness about parochial minds.

'I don't expect a single woman like you to be particularly sensitive to a young girl's reaction to an attractive and mature man like Gerard,' said Amy, with *hauteur*. She was obviously going to return blow with blow, no doubt to the enjoyment of the telephone operator. I determined not to be drawn. In any case, I had some gingerbread in the oven and it was beginning to smell 'most sentimental', as Kipling said. This was no time for a brawl.

'Look, Amy,' I said swiftly. 'I honestly think Vanessa is completely heart-whole – at least, as far as Gerard is concerned, so don't upset yourself on her behalf.'

Amy accepted the olive branch and spoke graciously.

'I hope you're right. You often are,' she added generously. 'I wondered if I should ring her at the hotel, but perhaps I'll wait.'

'Good idea,' I said, trying to keep the relief from my voice.

Amy, in meddlesome mood, is dangerous. 'No doubt, she would prefer to get in touch with you.'

'Yes, yes, that's so!' agreed Amy. She sounded thoughtful.

I rang off before she could start the discussion again, and made swiftly for the oven. The gingerbread could not have stood another two minutes.

I discovered, with some surprise, that half-term occurred the next weekend. So much had happened already this term, that I had not really collected my wits sufficiently to look ahead. What with Amy's affairs, the last trivial discomforts of my own injuries, Mrs Pringle's tribulations, the measles and the ordinary run of day-to-day school events, time had whirled by.

Miss Edwards, my infants' teacher, a pleasant girl who had been with me for two years since the departure of Mrs Bonny, brought to my notice the fact that, if we were proposing to have a Christmas concert, as usual, then we should start preparing for it.

She was right, of course, but the thought depressed me.

'What about a carol service with the nine lessons?' I countered weakly. 'We shall have the usual Christmas party in the school.'

She looked disappointed.

'Let me think about it over half-term,' I said, and we shelved the subject.

'And another thing,' she said. 'I'm getting married next Easter, so of course I shall give in my notice, and go at the end of next term. It's early to tell you, but I thought you'd like to know in good time.'

There was nothing to do but to congratulate her, but my

heart was leaden. I broke the news to the vicar when I saw him.

His face lit up with joy.

'What good news! She will make an excellent wife and mother.'

'There are too many girls rushing out of teaching to become excellent wives and mothers,' I said sourly. 'Especially infant teachers. Heaven knows when we'll get a replacement. After all, the colleges don't get the girls out until June or July. We shall have a whole term to fill in.'

This is a situation which has faced us often enough, but every time it brings pain and perplexity.

Mr Partridge trotted out his usual optimistic hopes.

'There's dear Miss Clare – ' he began.

'Much too old, and not fair to her or the children.'

'Well, Mrs Annett, perhaps?'

'She's two children of her own and a husband, and an old blind aunt coming for the summer.'

'Really? What a kind person she is! Lives for others, and an example to us all.'

I agreed. A heavy silence fell as we wrestled with the problem.

'Now, what about that good friend of yours who is so competent? The lady from Bent? She helped us once or twice, I believe.'

I said that Amy might manage the odd day or two, but was far too busy a person to commit herself to a whole term's teaching.

'Besides,' I said, 'Amy's methods are the same vintage as mine, and I think she'd find our infant room far too chaotic under today's conditions.'

'But I thought that was as it should be these days?' protested

Mr Partridge, looking bewildered. 'That last inspector who called – the one with no collar, you remember, and long hair – he said that young children needed to make a noise to develop properly. I recall his words quite clearly: "Meaningful activity creates noise".'

'So do other things,' I remarked tartly. 'The point is that to get a competent teacher for the infant room is going to be a headache.'

'I shall see that the post is advertised in good time,' said the vicar. 'After all, one never knows. Providence has been good to us before, and Fairacre is doubly attractive in the summer. I will have a word with the Office at once.'

'That might help,' I agreed.

'I must go and see Miss Edwards,' he said, 'to congratulate her. Are you sure you can't persuade your friend to come over from Bent for that term? It's not too bad a journey.'

'I will ask her, but I don't think there's much hope there. Her husband is recovering rather slowly from a car accident, complicated by catching measles.'

'Poor fellow,' said Mr Partridge sincerely. 'I heard he had been injured. He's lucky to have such a good wife to nurse him back to health.'

If he had added: 'And to his responsibilities as a married man,' I should not have been surprised. Clearly, the vicar knew exactly what had been happening at Bent.

One morning, during half-term, I was surprised and pleased to have a visit from Amy.

'Mrs Bennett's back,' she explained. 'Still a trifle wobbly, but it means I can get out now and again. James is in bed most of the day, so he's not in the way of Mrs Bennett's Hoover.'

She presented me with a splendid bunch of late chrysanthe-mums.

'By the way, you were right about Vanessa. She rang the very same night that we saw the photograph of Gerard and Hattie. I don't know if she was putting on a stout act, or whether she was genuinely pleased, but I must say she sounded so.'

I could afford to be magnanimous in the face of this.

'Well, naturally, as an aunt, you would be more anxious about Vanessa's feelings than I needed to be. But I always thought that Gerard's manner was more *avuncular* than *amatory*.'

'At Gerard's age,' commented Amy, 'it might well be both. He is practically the same age as James.'

We seemed to be treading close to dangerous ground.

'What did Vanessa say?' I asked hastily.

'Well, it seems that Gerard had confided to Vanessa his hopes of wooing Hattie some time ago. You remember she bought that house near the hotel? Evidently he was a constant visitor. Of course, all this is Vanessa's story, you understand. She may well be putting a good front on a somewhat humiliating episode.'

'I don't think so for a minute,' I said stoutly.

'He knew Hattie years ago. In fact, it was his friend who cut him out, so Vanessa says, which is why he's never married. It's rather romantic, isn't it, to think of him being faithful for all those years?'

'Maybe he didn't meet anyone he liked.'

'Trust you to throw cold water on any small fire of passion,' observed Amy, but she was smiling.

'I'm very glad it's ended this way,' I told her. 'Hattie May was always a darling, and the more I see of Gerard the better I like him. I look forward to meeting them both.'

'And so you shall,' declared Amy, 'for I'm inviting them down for a weekend as soon as James has properly recovered.'

She looked at me speculatively, as if weighing up something in her mind. I wondered what was worrying her.

'Have some coffee?' I suggested.

Amy shook her head.

'Not at the moment, thanks. I just wanted to let you know how things have worked out for James and me. You were such a help, when I was in the depths. It's only right that you should know the end of the story.'

'Amy,' I protested, 'there's absolutely no need!'

'Don't get alarmed! I shan't tell you any details that might bring a blush to your maiden cheek, I assure you.'

'Thank God for that! You know I hear far too many confidences for my peace of mind as a spinster.'

Amy looked suddenly contrite.

'I hope I didn't burden you too desperately,' she said, in a low voice. 'Perhaps I imposed on you as thoughtlessly as so many others do. I'm sorry.'

'Your troubles are quite different,' I said. 'And if two old friends like us can't help each other in a fix, it's a pity. You rallied to my support when I needed it. I hope I helped a little when things were tough with you. So, rattle away, and tell me what happened. Of course I want to know. It's just that I don't want you to feel obliged to *Tell All*.'

Amy laughed.

'Well, poor James has had long enough to think about things. I was careful not to press him too much. It was plain that he was desperately unhappy, and one evening after we were back at

home he volunteered the information that Jane's affections had
been cooling for some time. In fact, it was for this reason that
he had insisted on taking her away for the week-end to see if
they couldn't make things up. I think he was feeling pretty
silly too, as he had asked me for a divorce, and now the girl
was about to ditch him.'

'But surely, it would have been more sensible to have broken
with Jane then, rather than pursue her further?'

'Being sensible is not the usual state of mind when a man's
in love. Especially a middle-aged man. And you know James!
Love him as I do, I face the fact that he is a terrible show-off,
and always has been. The handmade shoes, the vastly expensive
suits, the fast cars – they're all the dreary old status symbols that
James loves to play with. They've never impressed me particularly, as he well knows, and perhaps that's where I have been
wrong – in letting him see that I have simply indulged his
weakness for his toys instead of letting him think I'm dazzled
by them. Well, we live and learn, and we've both learnt the
hard way these last few months.'

'It's over now,' I said consolingly.

'Yes, I think it is, as far as our natures will allow it to be. If
only we'd had children, I think we should have escaped some
of this damage.'

'There would have been other risks. They might have turned
out unsatisfactorily in one way or another, and I think that's
harder to bear than any result of one's own actions.'

Amy nodded and sighed.

'I suppose the old saying that man is born to trouble as the
sparks fly upward, is pretty true. However, our particular
trouble had a funny side.'

'Tell me.'

'Well, on the day of the accident, evidently, Jane was being remarkably offhand and James was doing his best to impress her as they drove – much too fast, I gather – down to Devon. According to him, she picked a quarrel about the best route to take, and was actually tugging at his arm when he was turning right, shouting that it was the wrong road.'

'I think there may be some truth in this. James isn't a liar about matters of this sort, and it's unlike him to have missed seeing the van coming up behind him. He drives much too fast, I always think, but he prides himself on being a good driver, and really he is.'

'So she may have caused the accident?'

'Who's to say? Anyway, she was furious with him. I heard a bit about her behaviour from the hospital staff. And she wouldn't answer the telephone when James tried to ring her. After some time, he began to accept the position, and it was then that he told me all about it.'

'Was he very miserable?'

'I think he'd begun to get over that. Let's say he was beginning to be more clear-headed, and to face the fact that he'd behaved badly. Also, that he was well out of a situation which would have been distinctly uncomfortable. Jane's mother, I gather, is a holy terror.

'Anyway, recovery was complete last week when a letter came from Jane. I've brought it for you to read.'

'Oh no!' I demurred. 'I'm sure James would be horrified if he knew you'd shown it to me!'

'Not he! Here, take it.'

She handed over the sheet of bright blue paper. In a large schoolgirl scrawl was Jane's final communication, presumably, to James.

It said:

"Dear James,

This is to give in my notice. I don't want to set foot in that office again, or to see you.

My mother says I should sue you for damages, but I've told her I don't want anything more to do with you. I must have been mad to waste my time with someone so old and dotty he can't even drive.

Jane

P.S. Yesterday I got engaged to Teddy Thimblemere in Accounts and we are getting married at Christmas."

'And how did James take that?' I asked, handing it back.

'He lay back on the pillow with his eyes closed, and then he began to shake. I was quite worried, until I realised it was with laughter. He laughed until the tears ran down his cheeks, and of course that set me laughing too! You should have heard the hullabaloo, and poor James gasping for breath, and saying: "Oh God, my poor ribs hurt so!" And me, wiping my eyes, and saying: "Try *not* to laugh, darling, you'll burst something!" And, after a bit, he would quieten down, and then remember some particular phrase like "so old and dotty he can't even drive", and double up all over again. It did us both a world of good!'

'Not enough laughter about these days,' I agreed.

'It's as good a healer as time,' said Amy, putting the letter into her bag. 'That little bout certainly restored us to happier days.'

'And so, all's well again?'

'As well as one can expect in an imperfect world,' said Amy. 'I daresay James will recover enough to turn to look at a pretty girl again, when he's had his nose patched up and a false tooth put in the gap. And no doubt I shall be as bossy and bitchy as I am at times. But somehow, I feel sure, nothing quite so serious will ever happen again.'

'I'm glad you told me,' I said. 'I like a happy ending.'

'Then let's have that coffee,' said Amy.

A week or so later, I was talking to Mr Willet in the playground after school, when a long low sports car of inordinate length drew up outside the school house.

It was a dashing vehicle, bright yellow in colour, with enormous headlamps and one of those back windows on top of the car like a skylight. The bonnet seemed about six feet in length, and the whole thing was dazzlingly polished.

'My word,' said Mr Willet, with awe, 'that must've cost a pretty penny! One of your millionaire friends droppin' in?'

'Strangers to me,' I was saying, when the door by the passenger's seat opened, and Vanessa emerged.

'Hello!' I welcomed her. 'How lovely to see you!'

'We're on our way to see Aunt Amy,' said Vanessa, kissing me, and enveloping me in fair hair and expensive scent. 'And this is Torquil.'

An enormous young man disengaged himself from the interior of the car, and shook my hand so warmly that I wondered if I should ever be able to part my fingers again. He was so good-looking, however, that I readily forgave him, and they came with me into the sitting room.

I thought I had never seen Vanessa quite so lively. It was quite apparent that Gerard's affairs were not worrying her.

On the contrary, she spoke of his marriage with the greatest joy.

'Wasn't it fun? That's really why he was off to town last time we called. He really deserves someone as nice as Hattie. He's so *kind*! I can't tell you how good he's been to me. I've *always* asked his advice about *everything*, and he's never failed me. And see what else he did?'

She gazed fondly upon Torquil, who gazed back in an equally besotted fashion.

'He introduced me to Torquil. And here, you see, we are! Just engaged!'

I hastened to congratulate them.

'We're not sure if we're on our heads or our heels,' said the young man. 'We rang Vanessa's father and mother last night, and we're going to stay there over the week-end.'

'And I said,' broke in Vanessa, 'we simply *must* call on you on the way, and Aunt Amy, because we wanted you to know before it was in the paper.'

'Well, I call it uncommonly nice of you,' I said, 'and I very much appreciate it. When will the wedding be?'

'Tomorrow,' said Torquil, 'if I had my way.'

'Dear thing!' said Vanessa indulgently. 'Probably early in the New Year.'

'As long as that?' exclaimed the young man.

I asked them to have a drink in celebration, but they looked at the clock, and each other, and said that they must go.

They fitted themselves skilfully into the gorgeous car. I kissed Vanessa, and kept my hands out of the way as I wished Torquil goodbye.

The car roared away. Mr Willet, who was carrying a bucket of coke to make up the stoves for the night, set it down, and pushed his cap to the back of his head with a black hand.

'You was cut out, I see,' he observed. 'That young lady saw him first.'

Sadly, I had to agree.

Three days later, Amy rang me.

'Have you seen the paper? And I *don't* mean *The Caxley Chronicle*!'

'Why? Is Vanessa's engagement in it?'

'Yes. Have you read it?'

'I had an accident with the paper today.'

'How do you mean?'

'I muddled it up with yesterday's, and gave it to the children to tear up for papier mâché bowls.'

'Really! The things you do! Sometimes I despair of you!'

'I despair of myself.'

'Well, listen! I'll read it to you.

"The engagement is announced between Torquil Ian Angus, only son of Wing Commander and Mrs Bruce Cameron of Blairlochinnie Castle, Ayrshire, and Vanessa Clare, only daughter of Mr and Mrs Charles Hunt of Hampstead, London."

'And will she live at Blair Tiddlywinks Castle?'

'Not for a long time. Torquil's father is in splendid health, I gather, and I don't think the banks and braes are altogether to Torquil's taste just yet. You know what he does?'

'No.'

'He's a band leader. And fairly rolling in money. No, I think London will be the place for those two for the next few years anyway.'

'Have they fixed the wedding date?'

'Yes. It's to be the first week in January. You're going to be invited, so you'd better start looking for that winter coat.'

'I will,' I said meekly.

'We shall be back for the wedding, of course,' said Amy.

'Back?' I echoed.

'From our holiday. James wants to go as soon as he's fit again, and that won't be long now.'

'And where are you going?'

Amy's voice bubbled with laughter.

'Can't you guess? To Crete.'

'*Perfect!*' I cried.

In a flash, I saw again that golden island, and breathed the heady scent of flowers and sun-baked earth. One day, I knew suddenly, I should go there once more.

'Give it all my love,' I said.